Cyril Abraham's
THE ONEDIN LINE
The Turning Tide

Bruce Stewart

A STAR BOOK

published by
the Paperback Division of
W. H. ALLEN & Co. Ltd

A Star Book
Published in 1980
by the Paperback Division of
W. H. Allen & Co. Ltd
A Howard and Wyndham Company
44 Hill Street, London W1X 8LB

Copyright © 1980 by Bruce Stewart

Printed in Great Britain by
Hunt Barnard Printing Ltd. Aylesbury, Bucks.

ISBN 0 352 305746

This book is sold subject to the condition that it shall
not, by way of trade or otherwise, be lent,
re-sold, hired out or otherwise circulated without the
publisher's prior consent in any form of
binding or cover other than that in which it is published
and without a similar condition including this
condition being imposed on the subsequent purchaser

CHAPTER ONE

A nameless green and yellow bird cawed from the tangle of an alien tree behind him. Far below, down by the blue bay, a harsh twanging and rattling arose, a sound that might have been taken for the straining of a stout ship in a gale had he not already recognised it as the music of the strange native people of this exotic shore.

Accustomed as he was to the dingy uniformity and strident racket of Liverpool (or the billowing of white sails and the howl of a buster), a place like this could never be home to James Onedin. And yet, he reflected, it is a place where money has been invested as calculatingly as it might have been in Church Street; where nature has been made to yield to industry as uncompromisingly as in Coburg Docks; where a dream has been dreamed and made to come true.

Port Baines. Deeper lines in his brow these days, his leathery skin tanned from his years in the sun, Captain James Onedin gazed thoughtfully down on the cluster of buildings huddled below him on the foreshore. Immediately behind them lay long, strong jetties stretching out into the fine natural harbour where the ships lay. There was a splendid array of them today, this day when his port, his creation, would finally be opened for trade. Every vessel of

5

the Onedin Line swung at anchor, called in to answer to the change in their owner's condition: friendly merchantment of as many nations as happened to be plying in the region: assertively flying the national colours and decked with bunting, a steam-powered gunboat of the Brazilian Navy, which only that morning had nosed through the heads, bringing interested businessmen and official government representatives from Rio de Janeiro.

James' eyes moved from the reassuring seascape to the green hills rising to westward. High up, the land fell suddenly away, dropping into a deep and misty gorge. Between the sheer slopes of this, a fine single-arch bridge had been thrown. It gleamed stark and solid in the clear, hot light.

'Port Baines,' murmured James Onedin to himself. And might have added without misplaced arrogance: 'My port. I alone have made it.'

A sudden little gust of wind broke over his face as he made his way down the rough track from the heights. That surprised James, for the day was heavy and still, and if he knew his South American foundation to have a fault, it was that the almost too perfect enclosure of the harbour by land protected it even from desirable changes in the weather. One missed the turbulence of the sea, and as often as not his proud white ships had to be towed out beyond the heads before they could loosen sheets and bear away.

'Papa,' called a crisp, youthful voice. 'What are you naming the bridge?'

A slim young woman stood across from him, gazing over the bay to the gorge with its dominating iron arch. She was attractive, perhaps beautiful, with dark and luminous eyes, and the bearing and manner of a woman well beyond her sixteen years. It remained a constant source of wonder to James that in his daughter Charlotte he could see at one and the same moment the child he had enfolded in his arms and the woman that was still to be. The woman was Anne, he realised: dead, remembered Anne whom he still mourned in his remote way, though he had now been married these four years to Laetitia Gaunt, once the child Charlotte's governess.

'The bridge,' responded James, halting. They were still high up, on a kind of ledge of land where the terrain flattened out briefly. Over the years of the building of Port Baines, James had taken to clambering up here alone in order to gaze down on his handiwork, like Moses beholding the Promised Land. At times of course, because of his natural pessimism, he had felt more like Napoleon regarding Waterloo. He vaguely wondered what Charlotte was doing here too. It must have been a stiff climb for her in the full skirts Laetitia insisted they both wore, though they were far from England and 'civilisation'.

'Well, bridges are usually named after the places where they're built, aren't they? You have the Tay Bridge or the Leith Bridge. This place has no other name but the name I've given it – Port Baines. As a result – '

'Oh, not Port Baines Bridge!' Charlotte gave a peremptory little toss of the head. She had long raven hair which flashed blue in the sun. 'Really, if much more is named Baines about here, the poor man will perish of delusions of grandeur. Have you seen the good Captain today?' she asked with a quick gurgle of laughter. Charlotte was an intelligent girl, and as a result of Letty's careful tutelage conversed well and with good intonation, but for all that she could seldom remain fixed in a mood for more than a few moments. 'Turned out in his best white duck, with a brand new cap and jacket, and an air of looking over his estate before the week-end party arrives. As I was passing him on Mersey-side, he suddenly turned on an unfortunate seaman who was tossing away a burnt-out clay pipe and roared at him he wouldn't stand for such filth and disorder on his ship, and by thunder, he'd better clear up the mess quick or he'd know all about it. He thinks Port Baines is a brigantine under his command.' She gurgled with laughter again.

7

Merseyside was the name given to the main thoroughfare of the little settlement, which ran round the horseshoe of the bay. It was a familiar and consoling designation for a community built up very largely of exiles. There were still hardly more than a dozen or so properly finished buildings, but tradesmen and small merchants had moved in over the years to cater to the needs of the work force. A town was unquestionably in the making. There was even a weatherboard civic centre where the Brazilian notables would later be entertained to a banquet, a place that Baines, who had now laboured on the port with James for a full two-year period, referred to definitively as the 'Town Hall'.

In his Moses-like mood, James Onedin could see a great and broad-avenued city here some day, a rival perhaps to the splendid Rio itself. But when he felt more like Napoleon, he would stare at the bridge over the gorge and wonder bleakly if that and that alone would prove his undoing.

'We could call it Santos Bridge,' suggested James. Santos was the nearest port, though without the harbour Port Baines already possessed and the shipping facilities it would most certainly have. 'Unless we want to forget all that sort of thing and name it in an entirely different way. We could even call it – ' He had a sudden inspiration, and almost laughed aloud with the pleasure of it. 'Yes, why not? You're concerned about the bridge. So we could call it – Charlotte Bridge!'

He encompassed the great iron structure with a wide gesture. Charlotte looked at him curiously sharply, then regarded the bridge again. James was at first perplexed by her apparent lack of reaction, but then understood that a completely new idea had been put to her, and she had decided not to respond to it with quick girlish enthusiasm but rather to consider it coolly. He rejoiced at this trait in her. It was one she had obviously inherited from him.

'Charlotte Bridge . . . ' she tried after a lengthy pause. 'It

8

has a nice sound, I suppose. But would people know why . . . ?'

Care. Caution. Qualities that James had found indispensible all through his career. Qualities that his daughter (for all that she was not the son he had once hoped for, and had even at the time blamed poor, dead Anne for not bringing forth) would carry on long after he, perhaps, had been found to have betrayed them.

James' pessimism returned as his gaze fell on the stark bones of the bridge again. It could look at times like nothing so much as a skeleton stretched across the gap in the hills. It was *his* bridge, built entirely with his money. Yet getting it erected had involved financial risk of an order quite new to him. It would take him years and years to get back in tolls what he had had to lay out, and for the moment he was cut to the wide, as good as busted, to put it at its highest an unattractive offer. It was not a realisation that lightened his heart.

The bridge had been absolutely necessary. Port Baines could simply not have existed without it. Goods from the rich interior might have been got as far as the hills above the bay, but there then remained the gorge, that sheer and unmanageable plunge between them and the land that sloped down to the sea. It had been James' hope in the beginning that the Brazilian government would help with the cost of the construction, but although there had been encouragement from the Emperor himself, the tolerant and scholarly Dom Pedro II, there had in the end been no financial aid.

The Brazilian government had extended the railway line from Curitiba to the coast. It had also improved the track generally. But when it came to so gross a matter as proffering coin, other considerations had begun to supervene. Foreign investment was welcomed in Brazil, yet the Emperor was no fool. He certainly did not intend to finance freebooters of another nation into positions which might prove to be those of princely power and influence.

9

'It's kind of you, Papa,' decided Charlotte at length. 'I appreciate you wanting to name the bridge after me. I appreciate that more than I can say. But as you've told me from the beginning, this is a business venture. So perhaps it would be wiser to think of naming it the Dom Pedro II Bridge. Or the Ysabel Bridge – after *his* child. Yes, that might be clever . . . '

My daughter, thought James solemnly. Anne's daughter? Once again the familiar, dead face became perceptible in the countenance before him. Oh Anne, Anne, am I to be forever guilty of your death? I know I never loved you well enough in life. I know I let you sacrifice your life to me, for no reward, for small comfort. But will you not now free me of you, and leave me to my new life with this child of yours – and Letty?

The wind was once more mysteriously gusty as James and Charlotte went on down the rough track. 'Is it going to rain?' asked Charlotte.

'I don't know. The cloud seems still, but at ground level it's fitful and blowy. Strange.' And then he asked her, 'Do you often come up here into the hills? I didn't know you liked getting away from everything the way I do.'

'Not in the same manner as you, Papa. Not as often.' She shared his need for high solitude then. Was that in the blood? 'But sometimes . . . to see the Indians.'

He frowned. Charlotte's interest in the *mamelucos* who were the natives of the area vaguely troubled James. He did not think himself a prejudiced man, but he felt the two civilisations were better staying out of each other's way: the *mamelucos* with their stone-age ways; the Europeans technically advanced and concerned to reproduce a modern world on this shore. There had been a tribe down by the bay when he had first arrived to make Port Baines. With kindness but insistence he had shifted them on to higher ground, building new dwellings for them, compensating them with gifts and goods, guaranteeing their much-valued fishing

10

rights. Now they only came down to spread their nets in the far corner of the bay that remained theirs, or perhaps to act as servants to those of the settlers who had residences. There was an Indian girl in the house James had built for himself and Letty. It was she, in fact, who had first interested Charlotte in her people and told her stories about them.

'Did you know the *mamelucos* are of mixed blood?' enquired Charlotte, gasping a little as they stumbled down the steep track. 'Derived from early alliances between the Spanish and Portuguese and the true Indians. Old Mecedo told me that the other day. The Indians' headman, you know? I'm learning to speak a little of the native language now. The *mamelucos* were so disconcerted by European ways that they reverted to primitive habits. So the Europeans began to think of them as Indians pure and simple, and enslaved them . . . '

Charlotte lurched forward with a cry as her foot slipped, and James had to grab her arm to save her from falling. 'I think that's the most awful thing of all,' gasped Charlotte, 'that there's still slavery in this country. In our day and age! It's against the Emperor's decree, against the Church, everything. But still it goes on. Slavery . . . '

James Onedin knew well enough that slavery still existed in Brazil. Not to put too fine a point on it, the local usage in this matter had at one time tempted him badly. Labour had been an expensive business all through the building period, and after a year or so of paying inflated rates to the itinerant workers whom he had had to import to help him, he had wondered if he might not raise a work force as simply and cheaply as it was said the developers of agricultural land in the interior did. It seemed there was little official interest as long as you were careful and discreet. What dissuaded James from the enterprise was the sudden (and in the event surprising) action of a British Navy vessel in arbitrarily seizing a Brazilian slave ship in Brazilian waters and refusing to release it until freedom had been officially guaranteed to the captives. It had been unlikely and quixotic, and had caused James to think again about what he had been proposing to do.

A twist of gritty dust swirled up abruptly from the un-paved road of 'Merseyside' before him, choking and half blinding him. 'I don't understand this weather,' he coughed to Baines at his side. The two men were approaching the tugs and dredgers which his sister Elizabeth and the Frazer Company had provided at the beginning of the Port Baines development. (Elizabeth had now married the knighted Daniel Fogarty and gone off with him and their boy William to live in Australia, where Daniel's extensive holdings were sited). 'Dark clouds on high, hardly moving, but turbulent at ground level. I don't recall conditions like it.' And then it began to rain.

Baines turned his grizzled head and large face up to the sky. The swollen drops, slow-dropping at first, splashed on to his countenance, his new jacket and clean white duck trousers. 'Been expecting something like this,' he observed phlegmatically. 'Stirred at first light, smelt a storm. Thought I was just dreaming, dreaming I was at sea. But I smelt her, sure as I smelt that blow long years back as did for the old *Orphir*. Times are, a man noses what's coming.'

'The old *Orphir* piled up because of a freak tropical storm,' commented James. 'We've had no warning of anything like that.'

'Started the same way,' murmured Baines. 'Wind playing merry hell with the white caps, not a breath up there in the tops'ls.'

They ran for shelter as the rain came down heavily. That savagery of the sea remains in his mind, thought James. He recalls how then his command was arbitrarily snatched away from him, and now he fears his day of triumph is going to be

12

wrenched out of his grasp too. James abruptly felt sorry for Baines as they plunged into a makeshift shelter erected near the steam cranes which would service the industrial end of the port. He and the huge seafarer were old companions, master and mate once, then owner and senior captain. Now they were – what? Partners? Twins of destiny?

The making of Port Baines had meant quite as much to Baines as it had to James. He had been absurdly pleased when James had first suggested naming the port after him. Then some notion of proprietorship, of belonging, had claimed him, and he had left the sea, insisting on coming ashore to share with its creator the three years of planning and toil it would take to construct the port. To James it was a business venture: to Baines it became in some sense the culmination of his existence. His name was here, so it was necessary that his sweat should fall here, just as one day he would lay down his bones here. It made a neat circle of life, instead of just a pointless straight line, teased out like yarn.

'All them nobs down there at the Town Hall,' muttered Baines unhappily. 'Wonder how they'll fare in this?' His unfamiliarly smart garments were bedraggled from the dowsing.

'Somebody'll get them in out of the rain, don't worry.' James grinned broadly. 'And you still look grand, man! A bit of a shower won't change our plans. I still mean to toast you as the living patron of Port Baines, and you're to reply. We'll cut along to the Town Hall as soon as this passes.'

'Out there,' said Baines. 'Look out there.'

He was nodding to the heads far across the bay, half-obscured now by the driving rain. Huge waves from the ocean beyond seemed to be rearing up here like sea monsters, lumbering with ever-increasing velocity towards the gap in the land. The waves were immense and powerful, and disintegrated in a great green and white explosion of spray

13

as they burst with shuddering force against the exposed face of the rock.

'The old *Orphir* was the finest brig I ever captained,' reflected Baines sombrely. 'If ships have souls, then she didn't ought to've had hers plucked out of her the way it was. Waves high as that, a mere few hours' fight . . . and then she was bones. Bones on a foreign shore. Something dies in a man too when that happens, Captain Onedin,' he concluded, still staring at the heads. 'Something's naught but bones in his heart forever after . . .'

James was flung physically against the mango tree, and clung to it for dear life. With the violent storm immediately overhead now and the great wind tearing bark from the trees, flinging fibre, earth, sand, and anything loose enough to be grabbed at high into the air, it was almost as dark as night. James had just left the Town Hall, which he and Baines had reached with some difficulty. They had found the Brazilian notables and commercial guests in a state of confusion and near panic.

'*Senhor Capitao, Senhor Capitao,*' a stout Portuguese in damp and soiled ceremonial uniform had wailed, waving his arms to no purpose. 'Where please in this wondrous Port Baines you have so marvellously constructed is simple protection from the elements to be found? You will observe the walls of this – ah – Town Hall. They bend. They wave like the sea. And the roof, *Senhor* – will it remain above us, do you believe, or will it crack and crumble, and before we can so much as entreat the Holy Virgin, descend on our unfortunate heads and destroy us without mercy?'

James ordered the babbling mob out of the swaying edifice and down into the excavation trenches of the pending warehouse complex. It might be wet there, but at least there was no danger of collapse. Urgent questions, demands, protests, flew about his head in at least five languages.

The ships in the bay bobbed like grotesque corks as he made his precarious way back along the sea front, some of them swinging in crazy circles on their anchor chains, like children's toys on the end of a string. He heard the vicious striking and grinding of timbers as two vessels collided, and just had time to think 'God above, is it a ship of mine?' before the wind howled furiously at him for such impertinence of thought and seized him up, practically throwing him into the water.

One of the long, strong jetties shuddered and groaned in agony as he battled past it. No, he prayed instinctively, remembering the arduous toil the sinking of the pylons had required, don't let the jetties be destroyed. Spare them, spare me that. A human cry rang out behind him, whether of terror or despair he could not tell and did not care. All his thoughts were now for the house he had built, and Charlotte and Letty.

The house stood on higher ground on the western side of the bay. Here not so many of the dense trees had been cleared, since it had been planned as a residential area. The huge *mongubas* that remained flailed and gesticulated as though possessed of demons. James had thought them noble and worth preserving when he had first set labourers to work on the plaster and tile hacienda, but now they were like monstrous devils out of the pit. A thick banana palm snapped like a twig and fell thunderously across his path. He leapt over it and raced for the long verandah of the dwelling, stumbling up on to it and pummelling at the heavy front door.

'Letty!' he yelled. 'Letty, for the Lord's sake!' The door fell back before his blows, creaking open. He was surprised to find it unlatched, but shoved powerfully at it, dashing inside. A vague clattering of objects informed him that the latch must have been forced by the buffeting wind and somebody had been vainly stacking chairs and suchlike on the other side of the door to keep it tight against the storm.

But a shutter hung uselessly on its hinges at the principal window, and the tempest howled into the room anyway. 'Letty – !'

She appeared, incongruously clutching to her a red glass lustre, an object which he knew she had had from her mother, and which remained especially precious to her. Her thin face was strained and pale, and there was a small blue bruise above her right eye. She had been sheltering in the inner room, trusting in the thick walls to protect her, terrified but trying not to give in to fear.

'Have you got her?' she cried. Her voice was hoarse, her eyes bright and wild. 'Have you got her?'

'Got who?'

'Charlotte! I've nearly gone mad worrying. She's not to be found, James! Where has she gone? Where – ?'

James stared at his wife. Distress underscored her bony, angular features. Letty had never been a beautiful woman: as far as her husband was concerned in fact, their marriage had not been one of attraction and desire, but of suitability. 'You mean Charlotte's not here?' he asked incredulously. 'Where has she gone?' Abruptly unreasoning anger overcame him. 'Good God, woman, what did you think you were about to let her out in a blow like this?'

Was not Letty still the child's governess? Did she imagine marriage somehow absolved her from the simple duties of guardianship? 'I've spent the last hour or so trying to batten down all over the settlement as far as possible! It's a hurricane, Letty! A damned savage hurricane! There may be men killed before this day is out. I promise you, if because of your negligence my daughter – '

'I couldn't stop her,' broke in Letty loudly. There was an edge of hysteria in her tone now and bright tears winked at the corners of her eyes. She had obviously been alone in the house too long, her fright building as the storm increased in rage and the wind in violence. 'She's a grown woman now, and won't listen when I chide her as she did in nursery days.

16

Won't listen, James! She *would* go. It was the Indians, she said, the Indians – '

'The Indians – ?'

'Would they be all right? Who'd see to them up there in the hills? I tried to persuade her that with their understanding of nature they'd be safer than any of us, but Charlotte – '

'God above!' A gust of naked fury, as abandoned as the storm itself, tore out of James. 'My child! You let my child go because of some nonsense about those damned Indians . . . ' He was trembling with a rage altogether foreign to him. Were the house to crumble and fall about his ears this instant, he would still speak what was in his heart. Who was this woman before him? What had she been before he had offered her marriage and a sound future? 'I will not stand for this flaunting of my wishes, Letty! You know how I feel about this interest of Charlotte's in the native people. I've told you how it angers me. But still you deliberately persist in – '

'I persist in nothing! Stop it, James! Stop accusing me!' She was shouting back at him, for a moment a thing of the storm too. 'I know I've never meant much to you, but it's evil of you to hate me so. Evil!'

'Hate you?' Despite the fury all about him, despite the sting of the driving rain still on his face, he was shocked. 'What are you talking about now, for the Lord's sake?'

'Oh, I know I'm not your precious Anne,' she babbled, crying freely. 'I'm well aware of it. I think I knew from the beginning I could never be.' She shot a peculiarly malevolent glance at him. 'Was that why you married me?' she demanded bitterly. 'Because you too knew I could only fail? Because you needed someone to confirm your fear that everything worthwhile in life had gone – everything except Anne's remaining gift to you . . . Charlotte . . . ?'

The wind clawed savagely into the room, grabbing at a bulky chiffonier, hurling it over as though it were straw. The distraught Letty barely noticed. And yet, James realised, that must surely be the worst part of all this to her. The destruction of her precious 'things'. Those civilised furnishings and ornaments that from the beginning she had insisted be brought, if she was to be expected to make a home in the wilderness. Letty was the slave of her society and its conventions.

'We haven't been very happy, have we, James?' she was running on in a flood of tears. 'I haven't made you very happy, if you like. But did you try to make me happy? Was that ever a concern of yours? I was just installed in your house, informed of my duties. Dragged halfway across the world when it became plain you needed me out here with you. Yet did you need me, James? Did you really?' Again the bitterness was in her tone. 'Or just someone to look after Charlotte...'

She was jealous, then. Jealous of his daughter. The wind howled into the room. And he understood that she was right, that in their few years of marriage he had known no joy of her. Again he was conscious of the sharpness of her features. Anne, Anne. Why did you have to die? Why should it be this unfortunate woman who suffers the worst consequence of it?

'A-hoy!' It was a huge, ringing cry, cutting across the storm. 'Cap'n Onedin, sir!'

James rushed to the gaping window. Outside in the swirling murk, a little group of persons was discernible. One was the towering figure of Baines. The other three were *mamelucos*, and they carried a prone figure.

'I knew as you'd be here,' shouted Baines above the roar of the wind. 'It's bad news, sir. Miss Charlotte – she's hurt.'

James raced outside, barely conscious of the gasping Letty on his heels. He recalled merely how when Anne had died, he had been angry and resentful to be left with a weakling girl on his hands. He recalled too how Laetitia Gaunt, coming into his house as governess, had slowly taught him how to love the daughter his wife had borne him. And now the

18

wheel had come full circle. Letty had come to feel a contempt for Charlotte; and he had discovered – yes, God help him, it was true – that his daughter was more important to him than the woman he had married.

'Best we get her inside, sir,' cried Baines as James raced up to the party struggling towards the verandah. 'Lucky I met with these here, or they mightn't have known where to come. She's passed out now. But before, she was coughing blood . . .'

James heard Letty stifle a cry as he stared down at the ashen, unmoving face of his child, the centre of his existence. 'How?' he demanded abruptly. 'How – ?'

'Couldn't rightly say, sir.'

'Them – ?' James swung on the *mamelucos*, shadowy figures like wind-tossed scarecrows in their ponchos and broad hats. His expression was suddenly ugly. 'By God, if I find any of them had aught to do with –'

One of the Indians gave tongue to some incomprehensible words. He had apparently understood what James was saying, but chose to respond in his own language. Baines, with his strange sense of comprehending what fellow human beings were trying to convey rather than what words in alien tongues actually meant, nodded briefly. 'They say she was climbing, sir. Up there in the high country. Only the wind took her sudden, and she slipped. The scrub and that held her, or she'd've crashed all the way to the sea.'

He jabbed a thick finger at the hills where James had been with Charlotte earlier in the day. James' eyes travelled to the ledge where they had stood and talked and the iron bridge across the gorge beyond. Abruptly he thought his eyes must be playing tricks on him. The bridge appeared to be shuddering.

But then it struck him with a thunderous shock that it was no deception, no quirk of the light and tempestuous weather. The bridge, the stark and solid bridge that connected Port Baines to the rich interior, was shaking on its foundations.

19

It was incredible. All thought of Charlotte banished from his head for the moment, he simply stared as increasingly violent ripples ran through the great iron structure. It was waving like a ribbon in the screaming hurricane. And then, almost as though it had been built of matchwood, it very slowly began to lift and buckle, the supports wrenching painfully out of the hillside, the disordered chunks dropping with agonising slowness to the gorge below. In helpless seconds that seemed like tortured hours, the bridge, his bridge built with his money, was being plucked from its ordained site and reduced to a meaningless tangle of un-identifiable metal, at one with the pervading, tossing, wildly waving green all about it.

The noise, when it reached them on the verandah of the bungalow, was that of a distant, absurdly prolonged ex-plosion. And James Onedin, shocked to his soul, could think of only two things. My daughter, Anne's child, may yet be a victim of this murderous hurricane. And I am destroyed, blown helpless on to the killing rocks. Sunk.

CHAPTER TWO

Lady Elizabeth Fogarty surveyed the familiar drawing room and nodded briefly. Nothing was changed in here. Though still under their dust sheets she could make out her tall Abbotsford chairs, exactly where they should have been around the walls, the elegant piano covered up in its corner, and a strange lumpy shape which she took to be the walnut credenza of which she had always been so fond.

Outside the big windows were the stolid residences of Prince's Boulevard, silhouetted against a blessedly grey sky. Elizabeth beamed at the gloom. It was not perverse of her. The fact was, she had enjoyed rather too much in the way of blue skies and bright sunshine recently. She could recall mornings in the spacious house Daniel had acquired in the affluent Balmain suburb of Sydney when she would wake up positively praying that if she were to rise that day, then heaven grant the sun would not too. Smiling heat was all very well in its way – and when she was being honest she had to admit that her husband Daniel seemed to thrive on it and their son William to accept it as normal – but there was a mysterious security in fog, murk, sullen clouds above and the blessed promise of chill rain. It was good to be back in Liverpool.

21

The squat housekeeper bobbed before her. 'Beg pardon, milady – was you wanting the tea served in here today then?'

'No, Mrs Eccles, I shan't be opening up this room again just yet. Nor the big dining room for that matter. Until further notice I shall take all my meals in the morning room.'

'Does that mean, milady . . . that is, as to the bedrooms . . . well – should I or shouldn't I . . . ' The dumpy little woman hesitated.

'What is it, Mrs Eccles?'

Mrs Eccles drew a breath. One of the disadvantages of her station was that the quality would never tell you straight out what you needed to know. And yet this woman before her was hardly born to genteel ways. She had until her marriage to the newly-knighted Sir Daniel Fogarty been merely a member of a mercantile family, rich perhaps but nothing special. So she should have been more understanding. 'I – I was just wondering, milady . . . when Sir Daniel would be returning.'

'Sir Daniel will not be returning,' announced Elizabeth briskly. 'Business unfortunately keeps him in far Australia. It is possible that Master William will be returning after a little, though. Yes, that is highly possible.' She seemed to ponder the matter for a moment. 'I'll let you know. For the moment there's no need to engage any more than the normal staff however, Mrs Eccles. I certainly won't be entertaining much.'

Mrs Eccles bobbed again and left. Elizabeth looked once more round the drawing room, and allowed wraiths from the past to rise up in shadowy life. She saw Albert Frazer in his favourite chair before the fireplace; Albert, who until his untimely passing had been her husband, and who together with his father Iron Jack had founded the prosperous Frazer Steamship Company. She beheld too the reception she had arranged for the mourners after Iron Jack in his turn had died, at which hard-headed Liverpool businessmen who

22

knew the terms of his will had finally acknowledged her as one of their number. She saw her brother James, soliciting interest and support for his South American venture, at the time something quite new; she saw her other brother Robert, influential at last because of his departmental store; she saw Daniel Fogarty – Daniel, returning into her life as a wealthy man, anxious to be recognised as the father of the child she and he had conceived years previously . . .

'Well, Daniel Fogarty,' said Elizabeth to the empty air, and yet not without a certain heavy emphasis, 'perhaps I was right to take pity on you, perhaps I wasn't. But if you only married me to get control of my son, then let me assure you it was a serious miscalculation on your part. The sort of miscalculation people are accustomed to make where I'm concerned. People like Chiara Santa,' she added in a lower tone. 'Chiara Santa . . .'

' . . . so he could be ruined,' declared Mr Tupman with an anxiety that was hardly natural to his business manner. 'Utterly ruined.'

'Bless my soul,' commented Robert blankly. His stout frame quite filled the *fauteuil* chair in which he sat. His successful and expanding departmental store had made him a man of substance in more senses than one.

'Surely you're exaggerating, Mr Tupman.' Elizabeth smiled gently. It was always necessary to demonstrate an inability to be dismayed before money men.

They sat in the upstairs office of what had once been the Salt Line headquarters but now housed the Onedin Line Ltd. Before going off to South America to build a port, James had modelled this office after his own personality. It had directness, purpose, his essential qualities of energy and industry. Such a man. But at the moment a man whose luck seemed to have let him down.

'I wish I were exaggerating, Lady Elizabeth,' Mr Tupman

resumed with a worried frown. Tupman, James' chief clerk, was older now and in a strange way less important-looking. Elizabeth had observed before that there are people in life who decline in stature as they appear to rise in the world. In this way Tupman was the antithesis of Robert. 'But at the moment it's simply impossible to say how much he's lost. All the costs of constructing the bridge haven't come in, you see. I was against him building that bridge from the outset, you know,' moaned Tupman, properly in mourning for the folly of a revered employer. 'Oh, yes. At his own expense. Outrageous. The bridge of course *had* to be built, but the Brazilian government should have been made to bear its share of the financial burden. The thing needed handling with delicacy and patience. If Captain Onedin has a fault,' pronounced Mr Tupman, now a headmaster rehearsing the virtues and failings of an old boy who had unaccountably finished up in the hands of the police, 'it is that he imagines he can solve all problems by his own unaided enterprise. He is an entrepreneur. A merchant corsair. I mean no offence by that,' added Tupman hastily. 'I simply point out that the very qualities which assure him of success are the qualities which can drive him into disaster too.'

'I wonder why James wanted to build a new port?' mused Elizabeth thoughtfully. 'He was never very clear about that at any time. Before I left for Australia, I even asked him if it was more than just expanding his business. If it was that he wanted to set himself up in another line of endeavour alto-gether. As a sort of – well, one-man Colonial Service.'

'Elizabeth,' interposed Robert disapprovingly. It was cold in the office. Yet he had proved in his department store that adequate heating was the touchstone of efficiency and profit-ability. 'Mr Tupman has called us here today to tell us that the family is faced with a grave situation. A very grave situation indeed. It isn't only James who is involved. It's quite as much you and me.'

'My interests these days are mainly in the Frazer company, which I administer for William until he is of age,' replied Elizabeth.

'That's as may be. But you still own fifteen per cent of Onedin Line Ltd., same as me.'

'Yet Daniel has an interest in Frazer's too,' continued Elizabeth with a frown. 'Yes. An interest which he will not relinquish. I find that strange. I told him from the beginning of our marriage that there was no point in his retaining it, as he was entirely committed to his Australian enterprises. I even offered to buy him out. But he wouldn't oblige me.'

'What's that got to do with anything?' snapped Robert irritably. He did not know why his sister was back in England at all instead of at her husband's side where she belonged. 'Mr Tupman,' he demanded of the clerk, 'can you not even say at this time what sort of figure James has lost?'

'I'm afraid it isn't as simple a question as that, Mr Onedin,' responded Tupman drily. 'The damage he has sustained in Port Baines may be considerable, and a great worry. But there is also the question of the payments to be met here.'

'Payments? What payments?'

'Payments to the bankers who have backed him,' said Tupman. He could be cool when he liked. Bad news disconcerted him, without doubt, but in the approach to dire prognostication he was calm. 'The venture in the end cost considerably more than Captain Onedin had estimated. That bridge in particular. He therefore instructed me to borrow here to enable him to finish what he had set out to do. To borrow heavily – and yes, it was the phrase he employed – at whatever cost.'

'He *was* making a colony,' nodded Elizabeth. 'Founding an empire . . .'

'Elizabeth, please!' Robert simply could not follow her preoccupations. And the cold in the office was quite severe.

'The entire company is mortgaged,' went on Tupman. 'The subsidiaries have been – ah – milked to provide what was necessary. And now, of course, we have this disaster to deal with.'

'Well then, how shall we deal with it?' Robert was anxious to narrow the debate to practicalities.

'I'm not sure.' Tupman sank to the occasion. He had wanted to be a lawyer in his youth, and indeed should have been, so delicate was his touch with tidings of great gloom. He picked up a cable from his desk top. It was one of many he had received in the past few days. It read, starkly:

SALVAGE OPERATIONS NECESSARY FOUR SHIPS SUNK TWO BADLY DAMAGED BRIDGE UTTERLY DESTROYED PORT BAINES IN RUINS CHARLOTTE INJURED ONEDIN

'It's extremely worrying about Miss Onedin,' murmured Tupman dutifully. 'Yes, extremely.'

'How badly is she hurt?' asked Elizabeth anxiously. This had been the matter of most concern to her too.

'Regrettably I have no precise details, Lady Fogarty. It is simply my understanding at the moment that Miss Onedin has been removed with all possible expedition to Sao Paulo, where she is to receive medical attention. But to return to these – ah – more mundane matters . . . '

Tupman laid the cable down again and settled back in his chair, pursing his lips and placing his long fingers together. The legal profession would never know what a natural practitioner it had missed. 'When there are debts of a certain order, it is necessary that there should be assets to support them,' he intoned, 'or business dealings cannot be sustained. When assets disappear – or as in this case are cruelly and without warning snatched away – the condition may be referred to as . . . why . . . '

All at once Robert knew that it was not the Liverpool

autumn outside making the room cold. The chill was of quite another nature. A gaunt spectre was reaching out its boney hand to enclose them all, and on its forehead was written the unlovely word: bankruptcy.

The hansom banged and squeaked along Water Street, hardly the city's proudest thoroughfare. What cobbles there were had sunk, leaving the surface scarred and pitted like a battlefield. 'I don't know what we're going to do,' remarked Robert for the tenth time in considerable worry. 'I simply cannot see what we're going to do.'

'Well, my dear Robert,' rejoined Elizabeth with distinct acerbity, crushed next to him in the confined space, 'if you don't know, there's surely no point in moaning about it.'

There was a particularly large jolt, thrusting them even harder against each other. Elizabeth wriggled free with an impatient gasp. Robert *had* put on weight. It was absurd. Robert for his part blinked at his sister. She held her head erect as always, and beyond the window that framed it a grey commercial world bounced by – warehouses, stacked crates and barrels, a skeletal horse at a trough. 'Aren't you the smallest bit bothered about this, for the Lord's sake?' he asked fretfully.

'I'm quite dreadfully bothered about Charlotte. She's my niece, after all, and I feel in some sort responsible for her. But I expect Letty will watch and pray over her, as she has done from the beginning. I must say I admire Letty,' added Elizabeth reflectively. 'In return for the security of marriage, she has agreed to bring up another woman's child. Not as governess any more, mind, but as mother. That's not easy. I'm not sure I could do it.'

Robert frowned. He was really too often at a loss to understand Elizabeth these days. Marriage was a *quid pro quo* as he saw it, and women anyway got the best of the

27

bargain. 'Why didn't Daniel come back home with you, Elizabeth?' he asked bluntly.

Elizabeth smiled charmingly. 'If I return to your house with you,' she asked her brother, 'shall I have the chance to talk to Sarah? We've really not exchanged more than a couple of words since I disembarked.'

'Why didn't Daniel come back home with you?' insisted Robert. 'Is there trouble?'

'What kind of trouble?'

'You know what I mean.' Robert was diffident all at once. He honestly had no talent for this kind of thing. Try as he might, in situations of delicacy he invariably sounded like the manager of an expanding department store hectoring a slack shopgirl. 'Marriage is naught but trouble and grief. Well, that's nothing to be ashamed of. You just have to face facts and – and act accordingly.'

'Things aren't going so well between you and Sarah, dear Robert?' enquired Elizabeth sweetly.

'I'm not talking about me and Sarah! I'm talking about you and Daniel Fogarty.'

'Daniel has his affairs,' responded Elizabeth enigmatically, 'and I have mine.'

If it was a dampening response, it was intended to be. Elizabeth gazed out the cab window. A section of the docks had come into view now, and she beheld the spars and furled booms of a brigantine towering over the squat black wharf buildings. Sail was not dead: no, not for all the 'tin kettles' at present under construction in the Frazer yards. James had always maintained that, and he had been right.

She had had the excuse of Frazer's and William's long-term interest for having to return to England, of course. Daniel for his part had understood when she had mentioned to him her obligations in this regard. There had been no quarrel: on the contrary, Daniel had entirely agreed that it was difficult, not to say dangerous, to try and run a company from twelve thousand miles away. 'And I'll be all right,

Elizabeth,' he had assured her with a broad smile. 'I really will be. You're not to worry. Just do what you have to, and try to enjoy it. Take as much time as you need.'

Yet had the accommodation been too ready? Had the smile been that fraction too willing? Elizabeth had found herself somewhat morosely brooding on these imponderables across the weary miles of ocean that separated Australia from England. She was forced to admit that she was glad to be away from Daniel for a while: marriage had created for her simple problems of proximity. It would have been different perhaps if William had wanted to come back with her.

William. His face came often into her mind. He was a young man these days, eighteen years old, tall and favoured, with a mind and money of his own. Daniel had made a generous settlement on him, anxious no doubt to compensate for what he saw as years of paternal neglect. Yet there had perhaps been more to it than that. Elizabeth could not explain why in Australia the impression had kept growing in her that Daniel had married her not for any virtue of her own, but to gain secure custody of her son.

But Australia in the general way had not been a huge success for Elizabeth. She had not in truth wanted to go when Daniel had said he must return; and then there had been the arduous journey, the burning climate, and the new society. Australia, though a British colony, was more unlike than like England. Daniel's knighthood had naturally made him extremely popular and sought after by the social climbers of Sydney. But this had only created further problems for Elizabeth. Missing her independence all at once, she had found herself a wife required to become a society hostess, being openhanded and charming to all sorts of wretched people. People like Chiara Santa.

'We'll have to sell our shares,' announced Robert abruptly, his bulk still jamming Elizabeth into a corner of the hansom. 'While they're still worth something. Aye. No sense in hanging on till the crash comes. We don't help James that way.'

'Well then, how *are* we going to help James?' asked Elizabeth, recalled. Chiara Santa. Really, the name sounded more like a wine. But if the opera singer had been a wine, she would have been a very bad year.

'Can he be helped?' Robert was glum. The loss of money and commercial standing were to him abominable things. Death was worse, perhaps, but only by a narrow margin. 'Brought it all on his own head. Would never listen, James, at any time of his life. Wouldn't listen to Tupman about that damned bridge. Was told the truth, but chose to ignore it. The whole thing was mad as rabbits from the start, and anyone could have seen.'

'He thought he'd build a town. Something bigger and better than anything he'd ever built before. More enduring. Something that would still be there after all the white ships in the register were scrapped or at the bottom of the sea . . . ' A beautiful singing voice, of course. The Australians, starved of such refinements, had been overwhelmed by it. The sweet songstress of Milano. The Italian linnet . . . '

'What's all this you keep saying about James wanting to found a colony or summat?' Robert's tone was prickly because he was perplexed. 'All James ever wanted was to make money for himself. That's all Port Baines meant. He'd no concern with setting himself up as king of the cannibal isles or whatever it is you seem to think.'

'Then why didn't he simply send somebody else out to make Port Baines? Stay here and run things? It would have made more sense. It was really too trusting to leave Mr Tupman in charge for so long, efficient as he might be. No, Robert. James went out to South America to throw himself body and soul into his venture. That was for something more than money. It was for true independence of purpose. The sort of independence of purpose that is allowed to women in our society only as I have in fact experienced it – before or between marriages. Women can't seek out destiny as James has done. They have it forced on them.' The Theatre Royal in Sydney had shimmered to Chiara's tones. What a night the opening of her *Traviata* had been! And when she had descended the staircase, candelabrum in hand, the gorgeous notes of *Caro nome* dropping like jewels from her lips, had she not been looking and smiling direct at the box? The box in which Elizabeth sat in the shadows with a bored William, her husband Daniel leaning forward, absorbed, captivated?

'I don't understand it.' Robert shook his head. The vibration of the cab exaggerated the agitation of his jowls. 'James, of all people, to be so foolish. To finish up like this.'

'James isn't finished!' Elizabeth found herself strangely sure of it. 'How can you say a thing like that?'

'It's not thousands of pounds involved, Elizabeth, it's hundreds of thousands. I saw the prospectus first off, remember, and I know the figures he was thinking in. Only thing that's different is that it's cost him even more than he thought. Poor James. He'll never hold up his head again.'

Never's a long time, Elizabeth consoled herself. Given a little enterprise – good will . . . She realised suddenly that she very much wanted to assist James, that she was prepared to go to some lengths to do so. She could not understand why completely, but she appreciated at once that it was not unconnected with Daniel. Daniel, who had once wanted to ruin James if he could, in vengeance for ancient wrong. Daniel, now the darling of that brash new world of Australia, responding to his naïveté, its enthusiasms, the visits of Italian opera sopranos . . .

The strange thing is, Elizabeth Fogarty suddenly thought, that I seem quite cheerfully to have abandoned my husband to that brash new world of Sydney. To that visiting Italian opera soprano. And that is quite unlike me. Quite unlike me indeed.

31

Lady Elizabeth Fogarty first made the acquaintance of the *Lady Elizabeth* one dank and drizzly afternoon when neither of them could have been said to be looking their best.

'There she is, milady,' beamed Hindle, the ageing yard master, indicating with his stick the black metal hull rising above its props and housing. 'Pretty as a picture.' He had been going to venture 'pretty as yourself done up for a ball' or some such pleasantry, but you never knew with these ones who'd gone up in the world. Old Hindle particularly didn't know about this young woman who was now head of the company he worked for and had thus had the next ship off the line named after her. He remembered when she had first come to these yards, on the arm of young Master Albert, God rest his soul. A wide-eyed bit of a girl she'd been then, only afraid she'd drag her skirts in the muck and get dirty. Little Lizzie Onedin.

'She's different from other steamships we've built here, Mr Hindle,' observed Elizabeth, casting a professional eye over the new vessel. 'What's her tonnage?'

'2600 net, milady.'

'That's light. And so narrow.'

'Makes for better speed. She'll do eleven knots, would you believe that? And steady, mind, steady. None of your lying about becalmed while mariners have to whistle for a wind, the way it is with square riggers. Especially in that there new Suez Canal, they tell me.'

Hindle was already a veteran of steam. He had spent his life in the Frazer yards, savouring the first successes of Iron Jack and his son Albert, enduring along with them the failures and miscalculations, even putting up with the hoots and jeers of drunken sail hands lurching out of the dockside taverns. All who worked for Frazer's had had to expect mockery at one time. Steam workers were the buffoons of the sea. But now they could point to the fact that their 'tin kettles' did three or four times the number of trips a year that a sailing vessel could manage, thus shifting three or four

32

times as much cargo and offering owners three or four times as much profit.

'What are her engines?' Though still herself a devotee of tall white ships, Elizabeth had an unforced interest in the enterprise she was keeping in good shape for her son. It was not just shop talk to get on the right side of the Hindles of this world.

'Triple-expansion, milady. That's – let's see now – 1800 horsepower. We've improved consumption of coal a good bit too. She'll need only twenty-five tons a day to keep her on the high seas, this one.'

Elizabeth recalled objectively that among the Frazer holdings was a Lancashire coal mine. That took care of *that* little problem. 'Who is she being built for?' she asked.

Hindle shook his grey head. 'Was to have been the Peninsular and Oriental. But they cancelled, wanting bigger ships. Seems they're thinking of going into this fancy refrigerator ship business. Think there's any future in that, milady?' Hindle did not wait for a reply. 'So the *Lady Elizabeth* will be a tramp. But a good one.'

'A tramp – ?'

'Begging your pardon, milady.' Hindle swallowed heavily. One sometimes forgot these ones as 'd gone up in the world could be offended by the new slang of the sea.

'It's simply that I'm not familiar with the term.'

'It's been coming in of late,' explained Hindle hastily, 'to mean a steamship as doesn't sail a regular route, but goes where the cargo's to be found. Big pickings in that, milady. Sugar, wheat, cotton even – there's times when there's so much of that class of stuff to be shifted, different parts of the world, that an owner's better off just getting his ships to call in unbidden, rather than fix them with a sailing schedule.'

'Well,' reflected Elizabeth, thoughtful again as she surveyed the dark hull surmounted by its slender funnels, 'the *Lady Elizabeth* is all dressed up with nowhere to go.'

'We haven't even got a launching date yet. But she'll find

a buyer, never you fear.' Hindle took her allusive remark for proprietorial concern. 'The world needs steamships so bad these times they say of folk like us, we just makes 'em by the mile, cuts off bits, closes 'em up with a few rivets, and calls for a customer.' Hindle cackled noisily. Lady Elizabeth did not join him in his mirth. That was the trouble with them as went up in the world too. No sense of humour.

'We'll launch the *Lady Elizabeth* as soon as is practical,' decreed Elizabeth with a sudden bright smile. 'I'll perform the ceremony myself whenever you find it convenient. And I shall accompany her on her maiden voyage.'

'Bless my soul.' It was all suddenly a little too brisk for old Hindle. 'Maiden? Maiden, you'd be going on? And where to?'

'South America,' replied Elizabeth glibly. 'I think it's time nations like – well, Brazil were let see what fine steamships we're manufacturing in England these days.'

'Brazil? Why Brazil?'

'Simply a goodwill trip.' Elizabeth appeared to at last take pity on the old man's confusion. 'There's a lot happening in Brazil, Mr Hindle,' she explained. 'A huge coastline to service. Then that great river of theirs that they've only recently opened up. The Amazon. I'm told it's so astonishingly wide in parts that it's like being miles out on the ocean navigating it.'

'But they've no coal,' objected Hindle. 'That's always been the trouble with South America and steamships. Never enough coal.'

'That could prove a disadvantage, true,' admitted Elizabeth, giving nothing away. Mr Tupman had wisely decided for the time being to make no official announcement about Port Baines, preferring to wait for a little and see how things turned out. As long as the necessary payments continued to be met, any suspicion would be allayed. It was when ready cash was no longer available that difficulties would arise. 'But doubtless if we whet their interest, they'll import larger

34

quantities of coal from the United States. Which *our* ships would then be needed to carry for them. Good day, Mr Hindle. I have many things to attend to. Thank you for letting me see how well things are going in the yard.'

Old Hindle scratched his cheek thoughtfully as she turned and moved away. She was a rum one, little Lizzie Onedin. Lots of the lads had thought Iron Jack a bit daft at the end to leave control to the likes of her. But there, she'd done well enough, if you overlooked she'd sloped off to Australia for a while with that new husband of hers. Business was steady. That about Brazil, though . . . Old Hindle sighed unhappily. If the worst came to the worst, he supposed she could at least bring back a cargo of nuts. They'd be in demand, come Christmas . . .

And Lady Elizabeth Fogarty, picking a careful way back across the noisome shipyard, knew at one and the same time why she was abandoning her husband to the brash new world of Sydney (with its visiting Italian sopranos) and why she wanted to help her brother James.

It was to restore a necessary balance to her existence. She had been an independent woman too long to settle down as the world now expected to a meek housewifely role, bravely facing up to the challenge of what seemed to be a too-conventional *femme fatale* of exotic origins. And she would not see someone destroyed who had set out to do as brave and splendid a thing as James had. To build a new town where nothing had existed before. To found a new human settlement. She knew that had been his ambition. And she would not see him ruined for it. Neither by his new misfortune, or by his old enemies.

35

CHAPTER THREE

'You've done a fine job, Baines,' said James Onedin in the smaller, less confident voice he had come to adopt since the winds of fate had turned so savagely against him. 'A better job than I would have thought possible. Certainly better than the likes of me had any right to expect. But . . . ' His tone was almost apologetic for a moment. 'Will she carry us there?'

Baines frowned darkly and set his square jaw. He did not care for this new self-doubt in Captain Onedin. In his mind, whatever the reverses of fortune, it was for men such as James to stand firm on the bridge, howling commands above the angry gale, while he and his kind looked lively and saw to it. It was strange how that relationship between the two of them had never basically altered, never mind that Baines was now a ship's master in his own right, and James merely a venal owner, sitting ashore, so the cynics said, living on good men's toil and counting his money in case it should ever grow less.

Well, it was less now. Baines did not rightly understand these things, but there were those who whispered that James Onedin and the Onedin Line itself were finished. Washed up. And all because of the devastation in Port Baines. The Captain had over-reached himself, and such insurance as he held would never cover the terrible damage. The huge grizzled seafarer shook his head dourly and glowered out across the bay. Port Baines. In some sort he supposed he must have over-reached himself too. Putting his name up as a name that all men should mouth for all time. Transforming himself from a mortal mariner into an enduring dot on the map. Pride goeth before a fall.

'That craft'll bear us to your chosen landfall, never fear that, Captain,' replied Baines gruffly, nodding towards the battered ship in the bay. 'I've been able to do little about the spanker aft, so we'd need to coax the weather like a fickle woman. But the masts and spars are as stout as they ever were, and yon's a brand new mizzen staysail, salvaged from one of the vessels as foundered. The damage for'ard don't account. She'd never stove in, come the seas of hell against her.'

'A crew – ?'

'There's them as died,' answered Baines stiffly, 'and them as sustained bad injury. We've done what we may about all. It leaves a dozen or so capable of working a ship, and anxious to if it'll mean hauling out of this place. I told them as we'll be hard to coast all the way, sheltered as any pleasure cruise. Those charts I had from the Brazil Navy afore they lugged away what was left of their gunboat show good channels and safe bays all along.'

Good channels. Safe bays. Yet could a bay ever be safe? James and Baines were on the foreshore of the blue horseshoe, before the ruined jetties, looking out towards the *Neptune*, Baines' ship. By luck or miracle, she was the only craft left in properly navigable condition. Despite her damage she still had a proud line, and could lift your heart with the hope of her. The aspect to seaward otherwise was grim. Flotsam from smashed ships washed against skeletal masts and cross trees protruding at crazy angles from a now calm sea. These were the corpses of once lively vessels, driven into the shallows and mercilessly sunk.

But to look to landward was to behold a desolation worthy of the Bible itself. The Town Hall, that vain and stupid boast, lay collapsed in a pile of broken boards and roofing. The dwelling houses, James' hacienda among them, were ripped of their tiles, their stout walls (built so as to keep out the unbearable heat) broached and crumbling. The tall trees and palms were snapped like giant matchsticks or absurdly thrown one against the other, embracing in the act of death. And down in the gorge was a sight a man could not bear to contemplate long: a mighty tangle of metal and debris, utterly shapeless, not a girder or a stanchion of which was any longer distinguishable or capable of being put to honest use. Down in the gorge was chaos come again.

'Will you want to go to Sao Paulo once more afore we cast off, sir?' asked Baines deferentially. 'I could maybe provision better if I had a few more days to scout about and see what's truly still to be found. Stores is scattered far and wide.'

'I shan't be going to Sao Paulo again,' responded James evenly. 'We sail on the morning tide.'

'Happen you'd maybe want to see Mrs Onedin and young Miss Charlotte a final time afore going north.' Baines shrugged, still unsure. 'We could be gone a rare old space ourselves.'

'Mrs Onedin will be all right,' replied James, a tension in him all at once. 'She was quite untouched by the calamity. It would take me twelve days, the best part of a fortnight, to get in and out of Sao Paulo again. Now where's the sense in wasting such time? Everything's been done for Miss Charlotte that can be. I spoke to the doctors personally. I'd only be held up. Held up when I should be about other things. Re-couping my losses here. Doing what I must do to balance the books.'

The nightmare journey to Sao Paulo with Charlotte and Letty came flooding back into his mind. After the hurricane, it had been immediately evident that Charlotte needed urgent medical attention. Yet not a ship in the bay had then been in a condition to carry them to Santos, from which port the journey to Sao Paulo, where the only hospital was, would have been possible. James had been at his wits' end until the *mamelucos* had come to his assistance, the *mamelucos*, who had known how to survive the storm as Letty had predicted, but who understood that Charlotte had risked her safety for them and now wished to repay the debt. It was an irony. An irony that James, distraught with concern, did not fully appreciate until later.

Charlotte coughed blood again as the crude donkey cart bumped them over the rough scrub country to the railhead. Her ribs were shattered, and a broken bone had pierced the lung. There was no train waiting, for the service to Port Baines had not yet come into operation, and they had to delay two whole days while a message was sent and a train returned. Then the journey in the stock car, with the Indians still in attendance, had been a further agony. When finally she had been got to the doctors, Charlotte had been more dead than alive. But the doctors had pronounced that the injury was not mortal and that Charlotte would recover, given long rest and recuperation. A thankful James had turned to the *mamelucos* to try and reward them for their devotion. But they had vanished. Assured that Charlotte would not die, they had melted away like mist. Only Letty remained. Letty, and out of the turbulence of the storm, the cold distance between them.

'Everything's being done for Miss Charlotte,' repeated James doggedly. He really could not afford to sink into sentiment. There were more important matters to concern him. Neither James Onedin nor his dependants could settle for a life of poverty and disgrace. Thus the payments had to be kept up in England to obscure the whole matter of the bankruptcy. A fortune had to be regained, or a sizeable proportion of it, by such means as these latitudes allowed ...

'I've taken a house for Mrs Onedin in Sao Paulo. She'll care for Miss Charlotte there 'til I return. In a family,' declared James authoritatively, 'it's the woman's business to see to the home and the welfare of those who live in it, the man's to go out into the hard world and turn the penny by which the family may live. Without which the family may *not* live.' And he gave heavy emphasis to the words, as though publicly and finally to indicate where for him the priorities lay.

Baines knew little about such things. He had avoided marriage all his life, and was glad of it. But as he gazed again at the *Neptune* – the dear, brave *Neptune*, all he had brought to this place and in the event all he would take away from it – he knew Captain Onedin to be in the grip of a fever. He had seen it ravage him before, when they had been (or seemed to be) so much younger. It was the fever for material gain, without which a man such as James Onedin could not live. The shipwreck of all his hopes had left naught but bones in his heart, just as it had been in his time with Baines and the foundering of the old *Orphir*: but that had merely made Baines sad and careful, whereas James in his disillusionment was bitter and wracked with anxiety. Profit. The Captain was desperate for his profit again.

'What's this place we're to fetch up in then, sir?' asked Baines. 'The Brazil Navy charts show all fine up past Recife, all the way to Para. But after that, there's little mapped. We go down river, you tell me. What's down a river for the likes of us?'

'It's not just a river. It's the mighty Amazon. And the place we're going – ' James stopped. Four men dead. Ten or so gravely injured. Good seafarers that one way or another he had brought to this corner of the world and their fate. That was what the folly of Port Baines had really cost. Then Charlotte's injury. It had cost that too. The discovery of how little Letty meant in his life. There was much to be atoned for. Much to be picked up from where it lay bruised

40

and helpless and set on its feet again. He needed his profit. And he needed it soon.

'The place we're going is the richest place in Brazil just now,' remarked James to Baines easily. 'Fortunes to be picked up off the streets. Manaos. A new, wealthy city, damn near a thousand miles down a river as broad as the Mediterranean. Where all I've lost will be restored to me. Manaos...'

The port of Para when the *Neptune* reached it was in festival, and there was nowhere to berth. The docking facilities were in any case primitive, but with the entire populace celebrating there was no one to service incoming craft. The *Neptune* lay out in the stream together with a schooner which had arrived at about the same time, but from downriver. As night gradually came down, this vessel remained darkened.

'What's the racket about again?' asked Baines, mystified as he blinked at the myriad lights and torches winking ashore and listened to the twang of the strange music and the whoops of the dancers. The British mariner was accustomed to Christmas and Easter and perhaps Whitsun as public holidays, but a festival at this time of year seemed out of all conscience.

'It's the festival of Nossa Senhora do Nazareth,' replied James easily, next to Baines on the poop. James had been ashore earlier in the ship's boat.

'Begging your pardon, sir – ?'

'Nossa Senhora do Nazareth. It means Our Lady of Nazareth.'

'Oh. One of them papist affairs.'

'It's the biggest festival in Para, I heard earlier. Everybody takes part. The churches start ringing their bells from first light, and after the processions and the services are over, it turns into a big celebration. They drink something they make from fermented *mandioca* root. I had a sip and it damn near blew the head off my shoulders. After enough of it, the women see it as their duty to make strangers – ah – welcome, they say.' James cleared his throat. He thought speculatively of his crew of a dozen survivors of Port Baines to whom only an hour ago he had granted shore leave. Would they survive tonight? It was noticeable that in the great blaze of light that seemed to illuminate the whole of Para, there were pools of discreet darkness. James took these to mark the town's many churches and convents. Religion and love: the Latins seemed to think of nothing else. Just as James thought of nothing but his profit, and how soon he might again enjoy it. But that was different. Different.

Baines turned away from the noise and the light, and leaned back against the poop rail, staring out over the dark water. It had seemed right for the Captain and himself to take the watch. Baines reached a chew of tobacco from his pocket, and bit off a hunk. That was one good thing about South America anyway. Good baccy. Good, plentiful, and cheap. Abruptly there was a glare of sheet lightning which turned everything stark white, and a ringing crack of thunder. Baines jerked his head upwards. 'My God,' he observed.

James was phlegmatic. 'We've had our ration of all that,' he returned, apparently confident that the fates had had their tax of him for the time being. 'It's been hot and steamy ever since we arrived. And the dancers in the town don't seem too worried. We'll get a downpour and there'll be an end to it.' He pointed a finger at the schooner across from them. 'Why doesn't that craft show a light?' he asked, puzzled.

Baines was looking out over the water again. 'I can't believe we're on a river,' he remarked. 'Approaching Para, we must have been seven, eight miles out. Yet even when we was tacking to make headway we never clapped eyes on the other bank.'

There was abrupt movement of some sort on the darkened schooner, though James could not make out what it was. The impression was of an appreciable number of people in some manner or other scuffing the deck timbers. It seemed odd that the crew should be swabbing down or whatever it was with no light to work by. James became more curious. 'Have you your glass there, Mr Baines?' he demanded, extending a hand.

All the way up the Brazilian coast from Santos, James and Baines had fallen effortlessly back into their ancient relationship. Nothing direct had been said, but from the moment they had hoisted anchor and cleared the chaos of Port Baines, it was clear that James was once more master of the vessel and Baines his trusted mate. All that was lacking was the tall hat, to be formally handed from one to the other as a badge of office.

But Baines' glass, rapidly cracked out to its full extension and handed over, showed James little. The schooner seemed to carry a full load, for she lay down to her line in the water. It was just possible to make out a couple of men going below. They looked like seafarers about their normal work, but of any kind of larger group James could distinguish no sign. Perhaps after all he had been mistaken. Also just to be seen on the deck was a quantity of folded material of some kind. From its apparent coarseness James would have taken it for sacking, but then its bleached colour put him more in mind of the ponchos the *mamelucos* had worn in Port Baines. Was the master of the schooner some kind of trader then? One of those who plied up and down the river, dealing honestly enough with those who could not be deceived, but defrauding the simple Amazon natives?

James had in fact seen the master of the schooner earlier. When he had gone ashore to discover if there was any way in which he might berth and provision his ship, he had come across him in argument with a bored and shabby soldier who seemed to be guarding the locked docks on this day of festival.

The military was everywhere in Para, though they evidenced little of the smartness and efficiency of British troops. (Despite his extensive journeyings, James Onedin remained in some respects essentially an Englishman abroad.) Following the revolution which had freed Brazil from the rule of Portugal, there had been a counter-revolution in the province of Para, which had had to be put down by the military. But even after twenty years the authorities of this vast and difficult-to-govern country seemed unwilling to relax vigilance.

'*Por favor*,' the master of the schooner was snarling at the sentry. The master was a short and unshaven individual, and by all appearances not lovable. 'I must get provisions for my ship. But in the town, nobody will sell me what I need.'

'It is Nossa Senhora do Nazareth,' replied the sentry flatly. He spoke with some resentment, plainly a man who found it penance enough to be denied the universal gaiety, and had no patience for the pointless complaints of a ship's master. 'Today you will get nothing. Tomorrow, tomorrow.'

'But I cannot wait till tomorrow, I must sail before that. I need *mandioca*, much of it. Twenty kilos. To make the *mandioca* cake, no? Then *pescada*. I need *pescada* too. You must let me into the stores of the docks.'

'I am not permitted to do that, senhor. There is no one there.'

James wondered vaguely why the master of the schooner wanted *mandioca* so badly, and in such quantity. He also wondered whether in fact the powdered root were a staple of victualling on ships in the area. *Mandioca* flour made a vile damper, *mandioca* cake, which only by the fondest imagining could be compared to bread. James had had occasion to be grateful that enough flour remained from Port Baines to have spared the *Neptune* the necessity of conforming to this particular local practice.

The evil-looking master of the schooner took coins from his pocket and jingled them in front of the sentry. 'I have money,' he grinned. He also had bad and crooked teeth, James observed. 'You see? *Reis*. Por favor. My needs are most urgent. You will let me into the stores of the docks, and I will take what I must have for my journey.' He grinned more broadly. It really was not a pleasant sight. The master of the schooner spread his hands in a genial gesture. 'Naturally you will write down all that I have taken, and on my return I will hasten to reimburse those to whom it belongs.'

The sentry, poorly paid, fed up with his job and the deprivations it occasionally subjected him to, would no doubt have accepted the bribe and complied. It would always have been possible for him to say afterwards that he had been dealing with a drunken disturbance on the other side of the docks when thieves broke into the stores and removed goods. But at this precise moment he saw James, only yards away from them.

The master of the schooner perceived a change in the sentry's attitude, and shot his head round. His glance fell on James and he seemed all at once deeply angered. He was plainly not used to being frustrated in his dealings. But the sentry could hardly consent to help him with somebody else looking on, so the master scowled contemptuously, spat on the ground and made off.

James supposed the master of the schooner to be Portuguese. But, as he had discovered on the journey up the coast from Santos, that sort of thing was hard to be sure of in Brazil. The country seemed not just a mixture but a positive tangle of the races. There had been the *mamelucos* in Port Baines – part-Indian, part Portuguese. In Pernambuco and again in Camocim James had met negroes, and here in Para there was a large population of *mulattos,* who were part-negro and part-white. Then there were the *cafuzos*, and the *curibocos*. But the *curibocos* were part-*cafuzo,* just as the *xibaros* were part-negro. All these groups were recognised as

45

distinct in their own way, but there was no precise racial hierarchy, as in Europe or the British colonies. Perhaps only the whites of European origin were very rich, but plenty of the negroes and other strains seemed affluent. The only ones who seemed to be truly trodden underfoot were the pure Indians, who lived a primitive life in the dense forests. Those who in one sense or another adopted their ways shared their fate. The closer you came to being an aboriginal of the continent, the more certain it was that you would be regarded as inferior, a threat, and exploitable.

'He's running up sail, sir,' announced Baines in some surprise. 'Look at that.'

There was another flash of lightning, and James, who had been staring at the glowing town again, blinked round in time to see the hands aboard the schooner peaking the mains'l, which was bellying out as it climbed the mast. James clamped Baines' glass to his eye once more, and clearly saw the squat little master of the vessel giving orders as yet another crack of thunder reverberated across the sky and the schooner came about and took a northerly heading.

'He must be in a hurry,' James supplied, puzzled. 'He could know all about it, quitting port in a blow like this.'

'Maybe he thinks he gains the advantage of a stiff wind. He's wearing ship to get away.'

'But he's unprovisioned,' frowned James. 'I heard him say so earlier. And still not showing a light – ?'

'Here – ' Baines pointed. A little catboat was now picking its pitching way out from the docks towards them. It was not very expertly handled, and as the sea rose and the lightning flashed again, it dipped and swayed, taking a full twenty minutes to get into the *Neptune*'s vicinity. Then it seemed uncertain of what it had come for. The catboat circled the area where the schooner had lain, then jibed over to James' ship and came alongside. It was a government patrol vessel, and there were armed soldiers aboard.

'Senhor Capitao,' called the officer in charge to James; he

was better turned out than his men and crisply authoritative where they were inclined to be merely officious. 'Where please is journeying this ship which had just raised anchor?'

'How should I know?' James called back. He jabbed a finger upriver. 'She's not out of sight yet. You could catch up with her if you've got anybody ashore sober enough to pilot a fast ketch. What do you want her for?'

'It is very serious,' shouted back the officer. He had obviously been carousing, or wenching, or both, and something had happened to drag him against his will from these pursuits. 'The captain of this schooner is carrying a forbidden cargo.'

'What cargo? Opium? Gold?'

'If he returns, be so good as to give what assistance you can,' concluded the officer shortly. 'He is carrying slaves.'

And James realised what the strange scuffing in the dark had been aboard the schooner. The master had been 'dancing' his slaves. It was for them too that he had wanted the large quantity of *mandioca.*

James realised further that the slaves involved must be Amazonian Indians, close relatives of the people his daughter Charlotte had so badly hurt herself trying to 'save'. The rain began. This time there were shouts and a dousing of lights ashore as the dancing was brought to an abrupt halt.

By chance, and to their immense surprise, James and Baines and the *Neptune* ran across the slave schooner again within forty-eight hours.

The mouth of the mighty Amazon river is not one mouth but several, because of the huge island known as Marajo which stands at the entrance. The northern part of Marajo is savannah, but the southern and eastern sections are dense forest. The *Neptune,* continuing on her course around the south tip of Marajo from the port of Para, was about to reach into the Tojopuru channel and thence into the

Amazon mainstream when James made a remarkable discovery.

He was scanning the coastline of the island with his glass, absorbed by the impenetrability of the Amazon forest. It was a way at least of taking his mind off his dire financial position, and the length of time it might yet take him to set it right. Trees seemed to grow everywhere ashore, and in the densest profusion. He had noticed the same thing at Para, where thick green hemmed in the town on all sides and new growth had to be constantly lopped to keep the forest at bay. James was examining one of the colossal trees which can grow as high as a hundred feet before putting out a first branch, and by accident lowered his sights to come upon a heavily wooded, sheltered cove. In it, her sails furled, lay the schooner he had puzzled about at Para.

'I'll be damned,' muttered Baines when James had informed him of this. 'Then he knew they were awake-up to him and didn't want to get caught if they gave chase. So instead of heading out to sea he sailed clean round the island, and stole in here. Crafty devil. How long'll he lie there with such a cargo, would you say?'

'Not long,' replied James. 'He's short of supplies, I tell you. Where's he away, that's what I ask?'

'Not far.' Baines in his turn was definitive. 'Maybe up to Cayenne, maybe never such a distance. There's lots'll still deal in slaves, in this part of the world. And lots of Christian gents buys 'em for cheap labour on their plantations, never mind the law or the Bible.'

James recalled for a moment his own temptation to employ slave labour at Port Baines. He was severely oppressed by his own circumstances at the moment: the oppression of others ought not to matter to him. Yet he heard his own voice propose: 'Why don't we show this slaver there's things honest seafarers won't stand for?'

Baines cocked a wary eye at him. It was a new sort of tack. 'We'd have to journey all the way back to Para to let

48

the authorities know, sir. And that'd waste time, such as you'd never have wasted even to go to Sao Paulo and visit your wife and child.'

James ignored the slur. 'It wasn't journeying back to Para I had in mind,' he said. 'Nothing like that at all.'

The ship's boat, with James, Baines and five hands aboard, slipped darkly and silently through the water. There was little wind, and cloud obscured the moon. It couldn't be more perfect for this sort of venture, thought James nervously, understandably tense. All afternoon, lying out of sight of the sheltered cove until night fell, he had been obsessed by the notion that what he was contemplating was ill-advised and pointless. It was his natural caution manifesting itself. Yet he did not intend to remain a cautious man in the matter of regaining his fortune: there he would be heedless, risky, and untroubled by scruple. So what was different in this case?

'What if they're armed?' It was a sharp whisper on the darkness. Baines was repeating a question he had put before but had not yet had the answer to. 'That'll turn into something we hadn't counted on, by God.'

'They won't be armed,' hissed back James. His confidence was aimed at the hands. They had come along on the venture reluctantly to say the least. Seafarers as a class simply find it hard not to do what their master suggests is the right course of action. They are used to putting their lives in his hands. That is why one of their names for him below decks is 'father'. 'What do men do who're laid up in a cove like this?' James went on. 'Men who've just missed a festival, all that drink and women? Why, they make up for it. They break out the rum.'

The shadow of the slaver was now looming up before them. She took some discerning, for she was again without lights. As they slid in alongside, a raucous, alcoholic laugh rang out above them. It began to seem James could be right.

4

Baines handled their getting aboard. Nobody was his equal when it came to the skills of the sea. Swinging the weighted line slowly and soundlessly in as great a circle as possible, at the precise moment he loosed it powerfully upwards. The smallest clank notified them that he had cast accurately and the grappling hook had secured to the rail.

They clambered quickly and cautiously up the rope. James went first. On deck as they reached it, everything was still and dark. For a moment James wondered if the schooner could in fact be deserted. But then the raucous laugh came again, and aft of them they saw the spark of a candle glowing on a barrel and three men hunched about it. They were indeed drinking rum.

Rifles, presumably belonging to the men, were propped up against a bulwark. Baines simply sauntered over to the group, seized up the rum bottle and shattered it over one man's head. He fell like a stone. The other two men jumped up, open mouthed, but before they could utter a cry, James had cracked a buckled fist into the face of one, and the other had gone down to a blow with a pin from the boatswain of the *Neptune*. They lay perfectly still on the deck.

'Now,' murmured Baines, approving the nautical neatness of the unconscious forms before him. He liked a tidy deck. 'Let's see if there's anything else left half alive on this tub.'

They went gingerly below, leaving a two-man guard on the hatch. Immediately below was the mess, and here a glowing storm lantern delineated the shadowy shapes of perhaps half a dozen men, variously passed out or collapsed over the table, a keg broached and empty near them. In a chair at the table's head slumped the squat, unshaven master James had seen briefly in Para. His mouth gaped open, revealing the broken and rotted teeth, and he snored thunderously. Again it was not a pleasant sight. The stench was suffocating.

'Makes you sick, don't it?' proffered Baines, glancing sourly around. He could be censorious when he chose. 'They were mine, I'd have every man jack up aloft and hauling on sheets afore he knew was it Christmas or Thursday. And any as tumbled into the drink 'd save his shipmates the trouble of sluicing the stink off him.' A half-empty flask stood on the table near him. Baines picked it up, sniffed at it, then, as though absentmindedly, slipped it into his pocket. 'So, sir,' he announced to James, 'them as would've made trouble is dealt with. We follow you.'

James knew where he had to go. The schooner was a small vessel, and there would be no place to imprison slaves other than the hold. When he and his men, encouraged now and newly confident, broke in the barred hatch, the odour from within was more than suffocating. Like the groans and weeping of the forty or so filthy, half-naked men and women lashed to the timbers, it overcame with its stench of cruelty, violence, and sad contempt of human being for human being.

They were near enough starved, but it had been found that the schooner was well-provisioned with victuals for the crew. Thrusting the still-unconscious master and his minions into the hold, lashed to the timbers like their captives, a group from the *Neptune* set about feeding the hungry. A breeze had sprung up, and while the bemused Indians ate, Baines piloted the schooner out of the sheltered cove and across the strait to the mainland. Here, equipped with a quantity of the material the vessel carried to serve for clothing, and invited to take their pick of anything else they took a fancy to, the Indians were released.

They made a dazed, still shocked group as they crept warily back into the jungle that was their natural home. They would somehow or other find their way back to wherever they had been stolen away from, or simply start life anew, hapless children of nature: until the next raiding party came, that was to say, the next white captain and his crew to enslave them.

For the practice of enslavement would not stop, James appreciated solemnly, as the painfully thin brown-skinned

51

men and women disappeared from view. The law and divines threatened sanctions temporal or eternal to no avail. But for the moment anyway, he, James Onedin, had put these people his daughter regarded so highly in his debt. That was why he had done it, he realised, and it was certainly better than him being beholden to them. Leaving the schooner, the evil master, and the whole wretched business of slavery to others to be concerned about, he gave the order to return to the *Neptune*. He, James Onedin, would proceed as planned to Manaos, the El Dorado of the Amazon, and there give himself to the much more urgent business of making money.

•

CHAPTER FOUR

The city of Manaos, when James Onedin arrived there, was rich, rumbustious, sprawling, and (though there were those who saw no reason to think so) in search of its soul.

It was to say the least a thoroughly unlikely place to find in the heart of equatorial South America. The long journey down the Amazon had been through country of almost incredible variety, but hardly such as to prepare the traveller for a brash, up-to-date city in the depths of the jungle. The *Neptune* had passed through barren, almost desert land where the broad river sliced the desolate Dry Campos region: had navigated seas, with quick and violent storms, in the vast expanses of water at both Obydos and the junction with the Rio Madeira; had kept well to seaward of cliffs as high as the cliffs of Dover, preponderous and dangerously eaten away by the powerful flow at Cararaucu. And everywhere the banks of the river had come into view, there had been the jungle. It crept down to the water's edge like a predatory animal. It was plainly more of a threat than the alligators that slid into the river all along its immense course. The war in this world was between man and nature, and only an inveterate gambler would have laid money on the proposition that man was remotely equipped to win.

James and the crew of the *Neptune*, finally mooring, simply stared at the secular vision that was Manaos. Erected on a tract of elevated land where the Amazon met the Rio Negro, the city was high and did not permit of conventional docks. Vessels calling there had to tie up to huge pontoons, sending their passengers ashore by small boat. A flying fox had been constructed to convey cargo up to the warehouses and dock offices, and its donkey engine chugged away all the time. Manaos had originally been founded as a Portuguese fort, but now seemed to have made up its mind to be a flamboyant European capital.

Progress was uneven, of course. The streets were in places wide boulévards, solidly paved, elsewhere potholed mud tracks. Noble and impressive buildings rose on all sides, flanked by squalid and rundown haciendas or the most rudimentary of grass huts. Gentlemen in black dress coats (worn in spite of the intense and muggy heat) formally paraded the streets, accompanied by elegant women and occasionally even a liveried servant. These would jostle incongruously with negresses in colourful robes carrying red water jars on their heads, or the *mulattos*, the *cafuzos* and the *cablocos*. These latter represented yet another racial subdivision of this extraordinary nation, and were in fact Amazonian Indians who had become 'civilised'. They knew little of their brothers in the dark forests. They were distinguished by their ornate earrings and heavy golden beads.

'Manaos is generous, Manaos is open-hearted,' beamed the effusive Italian, addressing James in a voluble patois, part-Portuguese, part-English, partly his native tongue. 'Manaos welcomes all. Especially the English peoples, who are so industrious and so serious. Per piacere – do you know Clerkenwell?'

'I was looking for one of those fortunes that's supposed to be lying about in the streets,' answered James grimly, seeing evidence of wealth in this place but not immediately how it was acquired. The white-jacketed, pomaded city

resident he was with had bounced up to James with infectious
geniality the moment he had come ashore after docking his
ship. It seemed to be the way of things here. People kept
an eye on the river, watching for new craft, hungry to latch
on to new arrivals. It was perhaps partly business acumen
(for the river brought or took away everything that was of
value here), partly the exiles' yearning for the breath of
home and civilisation. In any event, it was patently sincere.
'Only I suppose all the fortunes are under the mud today.'

'We will dig one up for you. You have brought an English
spade? English spades are fine spades. I wish I had many. I
could sell them all.' The little man beamed again. He was a
merchant, apparently well-placed in Manaos. Deferential
nods were accorded him as they passed through the commercial section of the town. Women favoured him with
smiles, though he could hardly have been called handsome.
'Per piacere. My aunt Rosa has gone to live in Clerkenwell.
It is a most healthful part of England, I am told. *Miserio*,
our family is now dispersed. Far and wide. When we had to
leave Napoli . . . '

His name was Juan Lombardo, a name which seemed in
itself a testimony to the polyglot nature of Manaos. He had
come there like everyone else in search of wealth, having been
forced to leave Europe because of economic stringency. The
area was fabulously rich and productive, yielding among
other things the best coffee in the world, vast harvests of
nuts, vegetable oils, jute, rosewood. The city was connected
by water not only to the Atlantic, but via the Rio Negro to
the Spanish republics of Ecuador, Venezuela and Peru. It was
an administrative centre too: the Emperor Dom Pedro II,
anxious to encourage development, had established a new
province of Amazonas with Manaos as its chief city. This
had meant a great influx of government officials. Most of the
individuals did not work, but occupied gilded chairs in the
new civic buildings attending to endless trivial formalities.

' . . . so what will you do, Senhor Capitao? In what sort

of business will you engage?' James became aware that the ebullient Italian was addressing a question to him. He had a way of talking that consisted in simply letting everything that was in his mind flow out at a great rate until something emerged that was more or less relevant. 'You have your fine ship. Do you seek merely to carry cargoes for others, or is it your desire to buy goods so that you may sell them elsewhere at a fine profit?'

'I need to make money,' responded James shortly. 'A lot of it.'

'There is much money to be made in Manaos. Some already have the *milhao*.'

'How do they get to make the *milhao*?'

'They work most hard. They think of nothing but money.' The Italian shrugged. They were crossing a bridge over one of the channels or *igarapes* by which the city was traversed at many points. These were to accommodate canoes, which nosed everywhere for the carriage of goods. A girl's faint shriek was heard as a long cigar-like shape vanished under the bridge. Well, perhaps not only for the carriage of goods. 'Work. The concentration on gain and more gain. They leave themselves no time for rest or enjoyment, senhor. For sleep. Nor even for love.' Lombardo shook his head, sighing deeply, all at once in profound depression. He would never make the *milhao*.

'Love can be a deceit,' replied James, his face serious. 'Love can turn out to be a kind of hate. You never guess that. If you ever think it, you think it's impossible. And then something happens – and it's plain to you . . . ' He paused on the bridge, gazing speculatively down at the water. It had a curious olive-brown colour. He was sorry now he had not gone to see Charlotte in Sao Paulo. Yes, he should have assured himself positively that all was well with her before coming on his journey. Not that he was not acting in her best interests by seeking urgently to restore his fortunes. He could not conceivably have waited about, doing nothing, until she was fully recovered. Women could come between a man and his duty to them sometimes. Women could turn him against their own welfare. Letty's face in the hacienda, the hurricane whirling about them, abruptly came back to him. He shook the memory away. 'As for rest and sleep,' he went on briskly, 'I've done without them plenty of times in my life before. And work – work is a necessity. It isn't arduous just because it's hard. Ask them in Liverpool. Plenty there'll tell you James Onedin doesn't mind how hard he has to toil. But he will have his profit of it. He will have his profit.'

Senhor Lombardo regarded the set, resolute countenance beside him, and was disturbed. He respected the English, as any man must who has learned what great things are the fruit of invention and enterprise. Without the English there would be no railway trains, no steamships, perhaps no iron and steel. But the seriousness of the English was sometimes hard to bear. He thought sadly of his Aunt Rosa in Clerkenwell. In Napoli she had laughed so much, everyone had remarked on it. Did she laugh any more?

'In what line, Senhor Lombardo, is there most profit to be gained?' asked James.

Lombardo allowed his eyes to drift away. Beyond them was a clear section of land, the forest having been razed and kept at bay, where nothing had as yet been constructed. 'Here will be the opera house,' he announced, indicating the open area.

'Opera house – ?'

'Si, senhor! It is part of the plan for Manaos. There is public subscription, and much money from the government. It will be a fine, a beautiful building – one to rank with the best opera houses in the world, and to which the greatest singers, senhor, will not be ashamed to come. Already – '

'Senhor Lombardo,' cut in James, 'I'm simply asking you – '

'Already,' continued Lombardo, not to be stopped in full

flow, 'singers come from Europe to delight us.' He could
hear familiar arias welling up. *Ah che la morte* . . . 'We can
pay the fees such artists command. Oh senhor, consider it.
When the cathedral is finally completed – Sao Joaquim – '
He jabbed a finger at a grandiose building in the course of
construction to the south of them. ' – and we have too our
opera house! Ah, it will be perfection. Manaos will be like
Napoli.' *Addio del passato, Questa o quella* . . .

'Damn it, I don't care about your silly opera house,'
interposed James irritably. It bothered him, talk of that sort.
He had come to Manaos because he believed it was a place
where men devoted themselves to the amassing of wealth
with purity of intention. Now this idiot of a merchant was
babbling on about tomfooleries. Once he began to make it
again, no jackass opera house would ever have a penny of his
money. 'I need to arrange my affairs here, and without
delay. I ask your advice, Senhor Lombardo. 'What's the best
business to go into to restore my fortunes?'

'Allora, if this is all that concerns you . . . ' Lombardo
shrugged again. 'Have you any capital?'

'A little. And I believe I shall be able to attract credit.'

'In Manaos, it is of advantage to have hard cash. Lay
your hands on as much as you can, senhor. And then, to
make money, a fortune . . . why – you must interest yourself
in rubber . . . '

Daniel Fogarty thrust down hard on the helm, and the boat
came sharply round on the sparkling blue water, heading
directly up into the wind. She was a smart little cutter, he
judged, and he was handling her splendidly. Sometimes
Daniel Fogarty missed the sea abominably. On days like
this, when a generous sun smiled down in the magnificent
harbour of Sydney and there was still wind enough to belly
out the sails and send a craft skimming across the white
caps, it seemed an odd quirk of fortune that had turned him

into a stolid man of business, stranded ashore with huge property and stock interests. The sun glared in Daniel's eyes, hot and bright. Elizabeth had not liked the Australian sun. He thrust on the helm again, changing to starboard tack.

A silvery laugh for'ard informed him that Chiara Santa and her associates were enjoying the outing. Dressed in their long, light frocks with hats securely fixed to their heads by means of pins and knotted veils, Chiara and three other ladies of the Carlo Mancini Opera Company clung grimly to the hatch surround, dashed by spray, half afraid, half exalted, the way women commonly are aboard small boats. Even in such unfavourable circumstances, Daniel could not help thinking, Chiara outshone her peers. Tall, with dark eyes that invited, and creamy olive skin of the most delicate texture, the opera singer was an outstandingly beautiful woman. She was back in Sydney after her prolonged and arduous tour of the other major cities. It had been triumph all the way. But Chiara had been overjoyed to see Daniel again, and had embraced him warmly, weeping tears of delight. He had found that surprising and moving.

On the other side of the hatch from Chiara clung William and two of his friends. William was a strong and independent youngster now, no longer tied to his mother's apron strings. Daniel recalled how before Elizabeth had travelled back to England (to see to her business affairs she had claimed, in a sudden and curiously unpredictable rush of concern), she had tried to prevail on William to journey with her. But William had refused point blank. The silver cord was severed. Not even pleas concerning the Frazer Company, which was one day to be his, could persuade Daniel Fogarty's son to leave his father. This did not mean that the two were particularly close. Indeed, despite all Daniel's efforts, an essential estrangement remained, dating from days when the son had not known of the father's existence. It was perhaps that William simply needed to convince himself that he had a life of his own, after so many years of dependence on his mother alone. There had been other elements in Elizabeth's departing for England too, elements that Daniel did not completely understand: he had received the distinct impression that she was weary, yet not so much of him personally as of the bond between them.

The jib swung across as Daniel again changed tack, and Chiara and her operatic friends shrieked and ducked as the boom lurched near, threatening to strike them. Daniel grinned cheerfully, enjoying their pretty discomfort, and Chiara shot him a dazzling smile. It once more surprised and moved him. He wondered idly how old Chiara Santa was. Certainly not a silly child, anyway: youthful yet mature, prodigiously talented, in the full bloom of her womanhood.

His eye fell on William, clinging on for dear life as the cutter now ran before the wind. His expression was not one of keen delight like that of the women. It was rather one of dogged tolerance and endurance. William Fogarty was not conspicuously enjoying himself.

A couple of hours later, Daniel was in his club in Macquarie Street reading the *Sydney Morning Herald* when William appeared and strode up to him.

'Father, I must speak with you,' he announced.

'My dear boy.' Daniel laid down his paper and beamed at him. With his crisp curled hair and his long, slender build William was a genuinely good-looking lad. Other club members, Daniel noted, looked round and nodded approvingly. The club was constructed in precise imitation of an English club, though the heavy and ornate masonry of the building did not accord any more than did the sombre hangings, leather armchairs and pictures of London on the panelled walls with the sub-tropical world outside. 'Will you take some brandy?'

'No, I want nothing like that.'

'Then sit down.'

William took the armchair opposite. He did not seem to

know what to do with his long legs, and tried them first in one unsuitable position, then in another. He kept shooting little glances over his shoulder, as though fearful he was being observed. He plainly had something to say.

'Well?' enquired Daniel, half-amused. He regretted he had missed the childhood of this boy whose young adulthood he found so pleasing.

'It's like this, Father.' William cleared his throat. He had acquired a little of both the accent and the attitude of the Australians in his time in the country. They spoke in a curiously flat way, seemingly unwilling to move their lips any more than was necessary, and could be direct to the point of rudeness. 'I'm worried about this opera singer lady, Chiara Santa.'

'Goodness me. Why on earth should you be worried about Chiara Santa?'

'Well, actually – ' William drew a breath. He appeared to be broaching a matter of some delicacy. 'If you want to know ... actually ... it's *you* I'm worried about.'

'Me – ?'

'Yes. I don't like the way she looks at you, Father.' William was abruptly earnest. 'I noticed it when she was here before, if you'd like to know, before Mother went to England. I thought then, I think now – well, she's after you ... ' He rushed on as Daniel gaped at him, resisting a temptation to burst out into loud laughter, 'Now I know you may think that's just silly, but she isn't married, Father, she's good-looking, and she is – well, an opera singer. You know what those kind of people can be. So I think you should send her about her business. You're still married to Mother.'

Daniel felt a little bewildered. He was not used to being advised in the matter of his friendships by his offspring, and he had not until now been aware of the pompous streak in William. 'I'm well aware that I'm *still* married to your mother,' he rejoined, laying the lightest emphasis on the word. Perhaps after all the silver cord was not entirely severed.

'Meaning you don't want to be?'

Daniel was astonished. 'What the devil do you mean by that?' he demanded. 'And what precisely is the matter with you today? Chiara Santa is an old friend. When she was in Sydney before, both your mother and I enjoyed her singing enormously. It's only natural I should look her up when she returns, take her out of the harbour with her friends and so on.'

'I thought it was her looked you up.'

'Whichever way it was, that's of no importance. What *is* the matter with you today?'

William stared at the floor a moment. He seemed uncertain. 'Mother didn't enjoy Signorina Santa's singing at all,' he said.

'Well.' Daniel found himself intrigued. 'She didn't say as much to me.'

'She did to me. And she told me that you . . . ' Now the tall young man appeared to find some difficulty going on. He bit his lip. 'She told me that you – well, that you don't even like music.'

For the first time, Daniel experienced a tiny movement of anger. The boy was now being offensive. Had they been at home, in Daniel's big house in Balmain, he would probably have shouted at him to put him in his place. But since they were in the club, where he was known and revered as Sir Daniel, the English knight who had descended with the charisma of his presence on the colonials, he spoke quietly. 'That will do for now, William.'

'But Father –'

'I said that will do, boy! Chiara Santa is a friend of mine, and will remain so.' He was still not raising his voice, but there was a distinct edge to the tone. 'You really needn't worry so about your mother. It wasn't my idea that she should go off on business to England. It was her own choice.

And you didn't choose to go with her. So that means we must both watch our p's and q's in her absence, no doubt...'

'Father, I didn't mean...' But William stopped short. He stared at the floor again, 'It's just ... when I was born – when you and Mother had me...' Again the boy seemed in difficulty. Despite his justifiable annoyance, Daniel could not help feeling sorry for him. 'I mean – you weren't married then...'

'No. It's true we weren't. These things happen in life sometimes. But I presume you don't regret having been born.' It was extraordinary. Where did his son get his pomposity from? His mother? His mother, to whom he was still obviously tied – ?

'What I'm saying is,' concluded William feebly, 'it can happen in that way on occasions. Between people who don't really think ... well, it can!' And he rose from the armchair, uncoiling legs that had somehow got twisted around each other.

Daniel was glad that he seemed to be about to leave, because he knew that if the boy remained much longer he would indeed lose his temper with him and possibly even strike him. Chiara Santa, he appreciated, was a singularly attractive woman. But there was the world of difference between assenting to an obvious fact like that and doing something about it. He still loved his wife Elizabeth. Or he loved her as much as she loved him. The question had not properly arisen.

William was turning to go. 'William,' said Daniel abruptly. 'Why didn't you want to go to England with your mother?' It was suddenly important to him to know.

William paused, looking back at his father with lambent eyes. 'You know the answer to that,' he replied.

'Because you wanted to be close to me at last? Make up finally for all the time in your life I wasn't there?' Daniel felt stupid saying it. Not only did he remain English enough to dislike sentiment in all its forms, but he was aware that the words embodied no more than a faint hope.

William shook his head. 'Because Mother was going to see to the affairs of Frazer's,' he corrected, 'which one day is to be mine.' He repeated the phrase parrot-fashion, in the tone of one who has been taught to mouth it whatever his personal feeling. 'But I've managed to forget all that out here, you know. All the damp and the smell and the squalor of the yards . . . You see, Father, I hate the sea,' confided William blandly. 'I hate the sea . . . '

And Daniel recalled what Elizabeth had once told him, that William, on being taken away at fourteen from training aboard *H.M.S. Conway*, had employed just those words to express heartfelt relief and gratitude. 'I hate the sea . . . ' And as his tall son moved away, still under his mother's spell though resentful of what she stood for, Daniel seemed to see again the dazzling smile of Chiara Santa, wind-blown, lashed by spray, happy to share with him the element he loved, and which had once been all his life . . .

'Do it, Captain Onedin,' insisted the young Englishman. 'Take the money and do what I require. It will only take a month or so. It *must* only take a month or so. And then you will have enough capital to do whatever it is you want here in Manaos.'

A firework went off in the night outside, describing a flaming parabola over the unfinished cathedral. There was a great burst of cheering and laughter. Every night at Manaos seemed to be a night of celebration, James thought irrelevantly. There *was* money in this artificially created city. Expensive food, clothing, even fireworks were all imported. Not to speak of the stone and materials to make fine buildings. Cost was no barrier. It remained a simple question of getting one's hands on some of the prodigious sums that passed over the money changers' tables.

'You want me to take you and your – ah – '

'Specimens.'

' – specimens back to England. For which you will pay me the sum of a thousand pounds.'

'Half now, half on completion.'

'It's good money.'

'I am not alone in this venture.'

In the other room, the tables clicked. They stood in an annexe of the casino, James and this young Britisher he had encountered only that afternoon. Large windows opened on to the hot, lighted town, alive with people, everything reflected in the winking river beyond. Portly little Lombardo, got up in his best, played roulette enthusiastically in the salon. It was typical of Manaos, James supposed, to have a casino before proper plumbing and sanitation. That sort of thing was a priority in most civilised parts of the world these days. But here, you could still find yourself as badly off in an emergency as when you had to unbutton in a typhoon.

'I'm not sure I want to return to England just now,' reflected James. 'Not even very briefly.'

'You fear your creditors?'

'I didn't say – '

'Captain Onedin, I am a man of the world.' His companion spread his hands deprecatingly. 'To be completely honest, I have heard of you and thus far followed your career in South America with some sympathy. It was a great tragedy about Port Baines. The losses must have been considerable.'

'I'll recoup them,' said James with determination. 'Every penny of them. But if I go back home, they could bankrupt me. And that would be the finish.'

'Not necessarily.' The young Englishman shook his head. His name was Henry Wickham, and he was an individual of wide interests and excellent connections. 'From what I understand, it's appreciated in financial circles in England that you have had incredibly bad luck. Out of diminished resources, you continue to meet contracted payments. You might find in fact that people were anxious to help you.'

'At a price. I know business, Mr Wickham,' James snorted. 'They'd take over my companies for a start. Leave me with the smell of an oil rag to begin again on.'

'What more have you as things stand?'

'My chances,' answered James, a little curious as to why he was talking to this stranger in this way. He seemed to compel confidence. 'While I've command of my own resources, I can make – arrangements.' He meant that he would sooner direct his own ruin, if it came to it, than have others do it for him. Like all true entrepreneurs, he believed he knew the uses of adversity. 'I'm used to settling my own affairs. Whatever form they take.'

'Anyway, my money can help you.' Henry Wickham smiled, coaxingly. He had great charm, the mark of his breeding. 'Come – a fast run to England and back. You can set me down wherever it suits. In a Cornish pirate cove if you wish. I simply have to get to London eventually.'

'Captain Baines could take you while I remain here and attend to my business affairs,' suggested James.

'No.'

'Why not? Baines is a master mariner.'

'I'm sorry.' Henry Wickham shook his head again, a serious and faraway look in his eyes. 'This matter is extremely important to me. I have made a judgement where you are concerned, and I will abide by that judgement. It is the nature of confidence. But I am not paying over a large sum of money – in cash – for a comparatively trivial service in order to be fobbed off with some other man of the sea, no matter how reputedly competent.'

James frowned. 'What are these – specimens of yours?'

'I am a botanist. I have various seeds and plants I have taken from the Amazonian jungle. It is more than a hobby, I assure you,' he added quickly, as James' expression became once more one of bewilderment. 'I have been here for over a

66

year, isolating exactly what I need. Now all my specimens must be got to England rapidly, the plants in a healthy condition and the seeds while they may still be planted and expected to germinate.'

'You mean – you're taking stuff back just to put in the garden in England?'

'The curator at Kew Gardens is an associate of mine. He will take responsibility in the matter.'

'But – ' James was confused and astonished. 'You're prepared to spend a thousand pounds over something as daft as this?'

'I am not alone in the venture,' repeated Wickham.

James Onedin wondered if Henry Wickham were after all soft in the head. He needed money, but this was like taking pennies from an idiot child. Any fool could have told the romantic botanist that the stuff that grew in the luxuriant jungle of South America would never grow in England. Things were too different. Try and make a banana palm or a *monguba* tree grow in Birkenhead, and the outraged British climate would kill it stone dead.

'*Capisco,*' nodded tubby Lombardo. 'You will go to England and return at once, gaining for your trouble one thousand English pounds. *Eccelente.* The promissory note of this Senhor Henry Wickham, together with the other securities you have been able to provide, will enable me to borrow sufficient cash for us to begin. In your absence, your – ah – friend and I will explore the means of procuring rubber in quantity.'

James looked to Baines, at his side in Lombardo's crowded office. The big seafarer was out of place and unhappy in such surroundings. He caught James' eye and seemed to plead for mercy. James heard his voice again from the conversation they had had the previous day. 'You'd never leave me doing office work while you've a sound deck under your feet, would you, Captain? I've no head for figures and that.'

'It's exactly the same as keeping ship's accounts,' James had responded dismissively. 'We can't both go with Wickham, and yet the commission he offers is vital to my enterprise. You'd be better employed . . . keeping an eye where an eye is to be kept.'

Remembering Lombardo's dedication to roulette at the casino, James had made up his mind that a bulk at least as solid as Baines' should stand between the Italian and what little there was in the office safe. It was hard cheese on his old companion, but there was no choice. While James scraped up the minimum cash to get started on what the Manaos locals called the 'rubber trail', it was necessary to have someone who knew the ways of business in this alien city. That someone was Lombardo. But Lombardo must be carefully watched.

The whole thing had sounded too simple to be true. Rubber grew naturally throughout the Amazon region, the product of thousands if not millions of trees. It was only necessary to tap these for their raw rubber, get the produce down river and thence to the world market. The profit in rubber was astonishing. It was in acute demand everywhere in the world, but only procurable from the Amazon. Thus rubber was worth whatever a shrewd trader felt he could charge for it. Even when the price was grossly inflated, European merchants would outbid each other for supplies. The only costs were the labour and transport required. The mighty river solved all transport problems for James, and he understood labour costs would hardly be considerable.

'Labour is cheap in Brazil,' shrugged Lombardo as James again raised the question with him in the dock office. 'Labour in the jungle, where you will wish it, is arranged through agents. The only trouble is, there is often not enough of it.'

'Not enough?'

68

'It is a strange thing.' Senhor Lombardo sat back in his chair and wrinkled his brow. 'Since the abolition of slavery in this land, the Indians will sometimes not work for wages. They seem to think it is work itself which has been abolished. We have had the Rio Branco Law of Free Birth recently, by the grace of our noble Emperor. This says that children of any remaining slaves will be free when they are twenty-one. And so *they* will not work either. Sometimes. Senhor Onedin, we are forced to say in Manaos . . . it is hard for a rich man to make a living.'

CHAPTER FIVE

When Lady Elizabeth Fogarty saw Port Baines for the first time, she wondered if she had crossed the broad Atlantic merely to clap eyes on the sort of squalor she could have ignored any day of the week in her own Merseyside shipyard. She wondered too if she had developed an antipathy to the sea, since throughout the latter part of the voyage particularly she had felt distinctly ill.

By and large, it had been a wretched trip out. The *Lady Elizabeth* had risen well enough to the challenge of the maiden voyage. She was a good ship. But she was constructed to carry cargo rather than passengers, and her narrow hull and bulky superstructure caused her to dip and plunge considerably. The turn of the screw, driving the vessel along at a constant eleven knots, sent steady vibrations through the metal frame. However, it had not been merely the motion of the ship that had brought about general ill-health, Elizabeth realised. A number of the crew seemed to have gone down with something. It was an unfamiliar fever. Even now, standing on the foredeck of the tramp as it lay at length in the still bay, gazing towards the confusion of iron and timber that scattered the shore, Elizabeth found herself again quite unsteady. The jungle, as always in this part of the world, had crept back where it had been cleared. The remains of the iron bridge over the gorge were already heavily interlaced with creeper, and new trees and bushes sprouted from the wreckage. It was as though Port Baines were an ancient ruin, long since abandoned by the race of men.

'We'll need to take on fresh water here, milady, even if there's little else,' said Blaney, the master, standing beside her as she surveyed the wreckage of her brother's dream. Blaney was a tall, bearded man from Belfast, normally as bronzed and weathered as any skipper of a white ship, at the moment grey and drawn. He had been ill too. 'And I'm worried about those hands from the black gang.'

'Captain Blaney, what is this strange fever?'

'There's them as puts a name to things, them as suffers them,' rejoined Blaney bleakly. Like most sailors, he entertained little regard for the medical profession. 'But I've two stokers down with it, and that's two too many. It's not every crewman can take on coaling the boilers. It's hard work, the hardest at sea, and a man needs to be solid built.'

Elizabeth reflected wryly that whatever changed in shipping, little changed for the sailor. Under canvas, men would be sent aloft in impossible weather to shorten sail, just as aboard steamships they would be plunged below to perform back-breaking labour in temperatures that could be as high as a hundred and forty degrees.

'It's when they start to cough it's the worst,' continued Blaney in a strangely remote voice. 'I woke up with the cough myself last night. I thought I'd crack clean in half, milady. I coughed up – black bile.'

Elizabeth allowed her eyes to drift towards him. He had been almost the first to fall victim to the fever, shortly after the *Lady Elizabeth* had called in at Kingston and then gone on to Belize to drop cargoes she had carried from England. All colour seemed to have drained from his face. He swayed as he stood on the foredeck. 'You need to look after yourself, Captain Blaney,' said Elizabeth. 'Perhaps you should hand over to Mr Prendergast for the time being . . . '

Ashore there were only a few *mamelucos,* come back to live in the bay itself since the new invaders of their land had vanished. One man had learned enough rudimentary English during the occupation to be able to converse with Elizabeth.

' . . . but I don't understand what has happened,' protested Elizabeth, her parasol over her head to shield her skin from the hot sun. 'Why has everybody disappeared? Captain Onedin – where is he? Has Captain Onedin gone somewhere too?'

'Captain Onedin – him go ship.'

'Where?'

The *mameluco* responded with a vague, tobacco-stained grin. It was dreadful the way they chewed tobacco, Elizabeth thought momentarily. She was sure it did them no good – nor the sailors who had picked up the habit from their like. 'Then the others. Captain Baines.' She tried to insist now. 'Did he go with Captain Onedin?'

Her question elicited no response whatever. Elizabeth began to be a little worried. Were these people cannibals, she wondered privately? Captain Blaney was only yards from her, seated on a rock near the ship's boat. He had utterly refused to take to his bunk when she had encouraged him to do so, but in his poor state of health he would plainly be of little use in an emergency. 'Mrs Onedin,' Elizabeth said briskly, in fact troubled to know what might have become of Letty. 'And Miss Charlotte. She was hurt – badly hurt.'

'Charlotte – Charlotte.' The tobacco-stained grin was wide and alert now. 'Good Miss Charlotte. Good friend *mameluco.*'

'The last I heard she was seriously injured. Can you tell me where she is?'

'Sao Paulo,' nodded the Indian. 'She go Sao Paulo. *Mameluco* peoples help. Because she sick, *mameluco* peoples make for Charlotte strong magic. She get well quick.' And he held out a kind of talisman slung round his neck. It was a tiny but rather too crudely depicted image of a woman. Elizabeth tactfully averted her eyes, but was grateful. At least these savages had eaten no one. Nor did they seem to be planning a banquet at the moment.

When the *Lady Elizabeth* got to Santos, where she would have to remain while her owner went inland to Sao Paulo, Captain Blaney was gravely ill and unable to stir from his bunk. He had finally succumbed to the strange fever. Elizabeth summoned medical aid and left the ship in charge of Mr Prendergast, the mate, who did not himself appear altogether a well man.

The journey inland to Sao Paulo was mercifully brief and involved little hardship. On the railway train, with the carriage window wide open, Elizabeth was agreeably surprised to find the climate less oppressive. It really had been so humid and sticky aboard ship and close to the coastline. They had been troubled most of all by insects, and particularly mosquitoes. Elizabeth rejoiced that these had gone, for the one or two bites she had had threatened to bring her out in unsightly lumps.

Sao Paulo turned out to be a much larger city than she had supposed, given for the most part to dealing in cattle, large consignments of which were brought from the interior for auction or killing. But at the modern hospital she could at first find no trace of Charlotte. 'If you please,' she demanded. 'Miss Charlotte Onedin. She may well be cured by now – I devoutly hope she has been cured – but I wish to know what has become of her. I am her aunt.' Elizabeth

73

was behaving precisely as she did to those who had become her underlings in England, but somehow it did not account. These people seemed to have no accurate notion of social divisions. They respected only money and the vulgar display of wealth, which she had been taught to believe were in bad taste. Thus it was some hours before she managed to get hold of an address in an area of Sao Paulo she did not know.

It was rather a run-down area, Elizabeth could not help noting with growing alarm as the conveyance she had hired took her deeper and deeper into the maze of narrow streets and high tenements. When eventually the cab reined to a stop, she could only think there must have been some mistake. People of the place were opening doors or leaning out of windows to stare at what was to them an apparition: a lady in fine linen alighting from a carriage such as only the rich used. She had plainly come to save her soul by the practice of good works. Would her charity extend to them?

A disconcerted Elizabeth found Letty on the second floor of the building she had been brought to. At first neither woman recognised the other. In a drab skirt and much thinner than Elizabeth remembered her, Letty was cooking something at a smoking range in the corner of a room which seemed to contain a cupboard, a table and some wooden chairs and not much more. As Elizabeth appeared at the door Letty looked sharply to her as though expecting some insult, taunt, or at the very least reproof. Then she realised who it was, stared a moment in disbelief, and burst into tears.

'Letty!' cried Elizabeth, shocked and stunned. 'Letty, what does this mean?'

'Where have you come from?' sobbed Letty. 'Oh, where? How?'

'Never mind about that. Where is James? Let me speak to him.'

'James is not here.'

'Then where is he? What has happened? I had no idea

74

things were as bad as this.' Elizabeth's eyes ran round the high-ceilinged room, an elegant parlour before the range had been added perhaps, now in appallingly bad repair, the plaster cracked, the floorboards warped. 'I was aware that the failure of Port Baines had cost James dear, but I didn't appreciate that it had reduced him to utter penury. Why didn't he let me know? I could at least have helped.'

'I thought . . . ' In the midst of her distress, Letty seemed deeply confused. 'What are you doing here? You – you went to live in Australia . . . '

It occurred to Elizabeth that of course, James would not have known even that she was back in England. She immediately hoped that her brother would *not* have tried to get in touch with her in Australia, describing his situation. Doing so would have alerted Daniel Fogarty to a changed situation, and perhaps encouraged in him certain wider reflections. It had been coming to Elizabeth on the voyage across the Atlantic that she really did not want Daniel Fogarty unexpectedly turning up in England to buy up what remained of the Onedin Line, in order to ruin James once and for all. She knew he still cherished that desire, out of ancient grievance. She wanted herself to set up with James in what would amount to a kind of opposition to Daniel. It meant no doubt she wanted to be her own woman again after the cloying constraints of their marriage. But did it also mean that she no longer loved her husband?

'Where is James?' asked Elizabeth again.

'James . . . is in Manaos.' Letty's grief brought out all the hard lines in her angular face. It again came into Elizabeth's mind that her sister-in-law had been a governess for most of her life.

'Where – ?'

'The city of the Amazon. Manaos. He has gone to Manaos to recoup his fortunes. He says he can do so there, and remarkably quickly. I had to remain and look after Charlotte. James left us money, of course. But it was not enough.

75

After the medical expenses had been met – living costs . . .
We had to move out of the house he'd taken for us. It was
far too expensive. And though I wrote to him urgently,
explained our plight – he sent no more . . .'

'James left you to your own devices?' Elizabeth stared at
the gaunt woman across from her. She knew James to be a
ruthless man, but for all that he had always in the past
shown due care and consideration towards members of his
family.

'I – I don't know.' Letty's rush of tears had stopped now.
She lifted her head bravely. There was a dignity and independence in her after all. A governess is one who has been
forced quite arbitrarily to occupy a menial position, Elizabeth reminded herself. 'I think – I think perhaps he just . . .
overlooked us.'

'That's as bad!'

'It's strange he overlooked Charlotte's situation. He
should have had everything to do with Charlotte in the fore-
front of his mind.' Letty's distress seemed suddenly close to
a kind of despair. 'It's different where I'm concerned, I
know. But for James, Charlotte . . . is Anne.'

Before Elizabeth could ponder this curious remark, the
door from an inner room opened, and a young woman
appeared. Again Elizabeth did not recognise her at once. It
was a number of years since she had seen her anyway, but
she had not counted on the new maturity in her niece, the
entirely adult presence. Yet the contours of her face, the
high cheek bones and dark eyes that might have belonged to
her dead mother put the matter beyond doubt. This was
Charlotte.

'My dear,' breathed Elizabeth. She could not tell whether
this self-contained young woman before her was in the same
distress as Letty or not. Certainly she had suffered – that
was in her face. But there was also a notable calm, as
though fierce storms had laid waste all about her but left her
basically untouched. She was serene. 'I'm so . . . Charlotte,

child, I'm so desperately sorry about this.'

She moved quickly to embrace her. The girl responded warmly, though with a little gasp of pain as Elizabeth tried to enfold her in a close hug. Then her aunt recalled having learned from the *mamelucos* that Charlotte had broken bones in the hurricane at Port Baines. She was obviously not completely recovered yet.

'Aunt Elizabeth,' said Charlotte. 'Will you take us to find Papa?'

Elizabeth blinked. The demand was so sudden, so direct. 'Why, child . . . you're not completely well yet, Charlotte. Anyone could see that. You need rest. As a first move, I'll get you out of this rat-infested hovel. What can James have thought he was doing?' She still found her brother's neglect of his wife and child perplexing.

'Papa hasn't forgotten us, if that's what you mean,' responded Charlotte gently. 'Letty thinks that, but it isn't true. He's simply too stricken by all that has happened, at his wits' end to know what to do for the best. So we must go and find him, and support him.'

'It seems to me at the moment it's his business to be supporting you.' Elizabeth found her perplexity turning to a kind of anger as she continued to look at this pale, unwell girl, and the thin form of her surrogate mother. It had really been the sheerest chance she had decided to leave England. They might have died before anyone could have known of their condition.

'Please, Aunt Elizabeth.' Charlotte was quietly insistent. 'We're all right. It's Papa who needs help.'

'Are you a saint, child?' Elizabeth was not surprised to find her voice had risen. It was too ridiculous. The girl had perhaps suffered brain damage in Port Baines. 'A willing victim? A fool?'

'She's Anne,' supplied a low, strained voice from near the smoking range. 'He left her too like this, once long ago. I heard about it. While he went off to make his fortune, the passion of his life as always. But she was still everything to him, even when he was behaving badly. And I am nothing. Nothing . . . '

James Onedin thought the bad weather no more than a squall to begin with. But as night came down over the wide ocean, the *Neptune*, weakened from her battering in the hurricane, began to sway and protest loudly as heavy and then heavier seas cannonaded against her bows and crashed aboard, spewing everywhere. James yelled orders above a howling wind and reduced canvas. Down to only the three topsails and the stay-sails, he brought his ship round and prepared to brazen out the storm. In his heart he prayed it was not a typhoon. They were a hundred miles or so east of the Indies, with no haven to run to.

Intelligence that the officers' quarters aft had flooded sent him clattering below to inspect. A lamp swung from the beam like a wild thing, casting a fitful and unreal light over the strange collection of jungle plants that sprouted here. It was hard to make out precisely what was going on, but a hugely concerned Henry Wickham was splashing about, up to his ankles in water, trying desperately with the help of two seamen to rescue his plants as they slithered uncontrollably about in their individual boxes and get them up into the dry on the fixed tables and chairs.

'We must save them from the salt water!' he shouted as he saw James. 'Salt water will kill them. Bear a hand!'

As master, James was taken aback to be addressed in this fashion, even by one who was commissioning his ship. But he was also confused by what seemed to be the order of priorities here. In a storm at sea it is customary first to think of preserving life and limb. Henry Wickham for his part was obviously more concerned to protect his specimens. One of the seamen, staggering to the table with a plant, slipped as the ship gave a sudden heave and lurched back, falling with a crash against the timbers.

'You fool!' shouted Henry Wickham, leaping to him and grabbing the plant from his hands before it too fell into the slopping water. 'Haven't I told you to take the greatest care with them? They are precious – precious!'

The little seaman was dazed and might well have hurt himself, but Wickham left him on his backside in the wet as he splashed with the plant back to the table and set it down, securing it like all the others within a fixed frame. The specimens waved and flapped like a miniature forest as the ship rolled heavily. It was grotesque and unnerving.

'You might have told me there was a danger of this happening, you know,' he cried at the still bemused James. 'I could have taken precautions.'

'Ahoy, below!' yelled a voice down the hatch. 'Tops'l away!'

James beat his way above again. The topsail was streaking out from the mast in the gale like a witch's cloak. Grabbing up the megaphone, James roared 'All hands! All hands! Stand by the jib! Sheets and braces!'

Tiny figures high above inched out on the pitching yards. If one of these were to fall and crash to a red pulp on the deck, James thought, would Henry Wickham consider it a lesser tragedy than the loss of one of his damned plants? The jib edged up, bellying as the furious wind caught it. The *Neptune* reeled and lurched, helpless in the tempest. She had weathered worse storms, James realised grimly, but since Port Baines she was a tired ship.

About twenty minutes later however the storm abated, and after fifty it had blown itself out entirely. Baines with his nose for a wind would have known what phenomenon of nature it had been. A *pampero* building up force as it moved westwards, perhaps, a buster; whatever you called it, James and his ship had been spared.

James clumped below again. The hands were cleaning up

79

the flooding now, but Wickham still fussed over his plants like a nervous mother. 'I've lost two,' he announced in forlorn tones as he saw James. 'I'm convinced of it. They were utterly soaked in brine, and more than likely will not survive. Good fresh water is always required while their hold on existence is delicate.' He turned his attention to the bruised leaves of a particular plant. 'Is there a possibility of further flooding?'

'You never can tell at sea.' Wickham was a cultivated man, and both by his presence on the ship and his conversation had begun to appeal to James. But his obsession could only be characterised as folly. 'What plants are these, Mr Wickham, that you choose to spend so much money and care on getting them to England, and would sooner see them live than the ship that carries them stay afloat?'

'Some are merely horticultural curiosities,' responded Wickham, ignoring the sarcasm, 'which may be of interest to my associate at Kew Gardens. The *iriartea ventricosa* here, for example.' He indicated a small sprout that already bore tiny palm leaves, and then smiled a quick apology for the latinism. 'Better known as the bulging-stemmed palm. It grows to a height of perhaps fifty feet, and at regular intervals in the trunk puts forth curious bulges. Then the *desmoncus . . .* ' He grinned more broadly. 'But the majority of the plants are more practical than that. The majority belong to a particular useful species which I am anxious to get to England.' He swept a hand over the crammed table and elevated portions of the cabin, where there must now have been some thirty or forty growths. 'Twenty-five of these plants are identical, though at this stage they may not look it. And I have hundreds of seeds of the same ready to be germinated at home.'

'What species are they?' asked James.

Henry Wickham looked up from the plant he had been tending. In his eyes was the faraway look once more. 'Sometimes I feel like a botanical pioneer,' he returned. 'Like

Bligh. You've heard of Captain Bligh?'

'Him whose ship was taken from him by mutineers?' returned James in some surprise. 'I see nothing to envy in being like him.'

'The mutiny was an unfortunate blemish on an otherwise excellent man's reputation,' observed Wickham moderately. 'Bligh's true achievement while at sea had been transporting breadfruit plants from the South Seas to those same Indies we have just left. They have survived and prospered there. They still feed a large proportion of the populace.'

'And what do you take back to England, Mr Wickham? Something that will sprout porridge for the starving English poor?' James felt he could joke safely enough with the botanist. He did not seem to take offence easily, and perhaps needed to be put in his place from time to time.

'Not quite that, I fear,' replied Wickham very seriously. 'Have you a family, Captain Onedin?'

'A family?' James frowned, taken aback by the question. 'Aye. Aye, I've a wife and child.' Letty's face returned to him, Letty's face in the hurricane and Charlotte's when she was injured. It was ridiculous to be distracted by thoughts of the two of them, as he had found himself being more and more as he journeyed. He had seen to them well. 'Why do you ask, sir?'

'Because a family man might be expected to have the prosperity of the English nation at heart,' stated Wickham. 'As I have. That is why I am transporting to my native land ... rubber tree plants.'

James believed he had misheard. The *Neptune* still creaked and groaned and the word might well have been smothered by a large protest. But Wickham repeated quite clearly, 'Rubber tree plants.'

Now James knew for certain that Henry Wickham was unhinged. It was an almost alarming coincidence that he should be raising part of the capital needed for his investment in the rubber trade in Brazil by carrying back to England rubber tree plants that could only conceivably perish. Even under hothouse conditions they could not be expected to prosper. England would never become a producer of rubber. The thing was absurd.

James Onedin had once before built his fortune on a dream of his own, a dream about ships and the sea and the world-wide expansion of trade. He was building his second fortune on another man's dream, a dream that must surely burst like a soap bubble.

'But it's tragic,' wept Elizabeth Fogarty. 'Utterly tragic!'

It was not that she grieved so profoundly for Captain Blaney. Before he had been called upon to skipper the *Lady Elizabeth* on her maiden voyage, she had barely known of his existence. But for a man to die so, far from home in a foreign land, was deeply disturbing. It was the more shocking to reflect that it could have been she herself. Elizabeth had returned to Santos with Letty and Charlotte to grim news. Blaney had perished and most of the rest of the ship's company was gravely ill.

'You were lucky to have been spared, Lady Elizabeth,' said the ageing medical man soberly, voicing her thoughts. 'Your ship has been incubating yellow fever.'

'Yellow fever!' The very word filled Elizabeth with terror.

'If you yourself have not by now suffered high temperatures, retching and the emission of black bile, then there is probably nothing to worry about,' continued the medical man remarkably objectively. He was a white-haired Scot who had years ago married a woman of Santos and come to live in these parts, making the ships that called in and their crews his main practice. 'May I ask if you were bitten by mosquitoes?'

'A couple of times. There seemed a lot aboard ship on the last leg of our voyage.'

82

'Then in my view you were extremely lucky.' The Scottish doctor nodded sagely. He maintained a tiny surgery on the docks, and it was here that they sat and talked. 'We know very little about yellow fever. But there was a barrel of water aboard the *Lady Elizabeth* in which mosquitoes were breeding. A member of the crew told me it was a consignment taken aboard at Kingston.'

'That's so,' confirmed Elizabeth. 'We still had drinking water enough when we'd crossed the Atlantic, but we were short of water for other purposes. But are you telling me, Doctor . . . are you saying that yellow fever is in some way *caused* by mosquitoes?'

The elderly Scot shook his head slowly. He could not answer such questions. Nobody could with any confidence. 'I only know this,' he replied ruminatively. 'Years ago now, a trader visited some primitive people on the coast of Paranagua. They particularly admired a large drinking vessel that he had aboard ship. He gladly traded it, though it seemed the vessel still contained some stale water when he handed it over. The natives put it on display in a special place, a venerated and prized object. Less than a month later, the entire village had died of yellow fever.'

Elizabeth gazed out the office window at the funnels and stacks of the ships in harbour. Though coal was a problem in Brazil generally, it did not seem to dampen the enthusiasm for steamships. There was only one tall, clean mast rising above the squat, grimy tramps. It pointed to the heavens as solemnly as a church spire: an inspiration, a reproach. 'How long will it take for my crew to be back on its feet again?' she asked.

'Some may never be. I think it only fair to warn you, Lady Elizabeth, that there may be more deaths.'

'But for those who will recover?'

'Many weeks. Perhaps months. There is no precise cure for the disease, and regaining strength after such a sapping illness is a lengthy business.'

83

'I can't wait that long,' said Elizabeth. She could be as impatient as James when she wanted to be, and as cool in the face of human suffering. 'I will see to it that the sick are properly lodged and cared for, and I will recruit a new crew. I take it the barrel in which the mosquitoes were breeding has been removed from the ship? A search made to see there are no further such breeding grounds? In case you are right, Doctor, we must take no chances.'

The Scots doctor thought the titled English lady before him neither hard nor heartless. In a long life of condemning to as peaceful a death as possible those who came to him for a cure, he had become a realist too. But he wished somebody would investigate his suspicions about mosquitoes and yellow fever. Of course it was a vain hope, but if he were proved right his name could finish up in the medical books. Along with Jenner. Harvey ...

'I fear I do not speak Portuguese,' proclaimed Elizabeth loudly, as though volume might make her meaning clear to the short and unshaven ship's master who regarded her with beady eyes. 'I am simply saying that I need a captain and crew to take me and my ship to Manaos.'

'Manaos.' The squalid little man nodded vigorously, and the beady eyes lit up. He seemed to smell a little, but Elizabeth had found that was completely normal for people in this remote land. The plumbing and sewage, she had noticed, were everywhere in a primitive condition. 'Manaos. Si, si. *Bello*.'

'If you would permit me, Aunt Elizabeth,' interposed Charlotte with a smile. She rose from the chair where she had been sitting next to Elizabeth, and began to address the seafarer in hesitant but confident Portuguese. Elizabeth was to say the least intrigued. Charlotte seemed to possess a number of abilities which had been either forbidden or out of the question to young women when she had been her age.

84

Charlotte on the whole seemed a remarkable young woman. She had told Elizabeth of her interest in the Indian people of the vast country, and apparently she had mastered some of their language too. She had devoted her long and in the end poverty-stricken convalescence to the study of tongues, indigenous customs and other things like native food and drink. She appeared to have suffered few ill effects of either injury or penury. A good meal and decent surroundings once more had seemed quite to restore her spirits. The only thing she had continued to ask was that they should as soon as possible go to her father's 'rescue'.

Elizabeth had found that the more extraordinary the more she thought of it. Charlotte was an Onedin of course, and blood is thicker than water. But she was intelligent, and did not appear to make her judgements on emotional grounds. In fact there was something a little chill and detached about her in this area. James was like that. But did Charlotte despise Letty, Elizabeth wondered vaguely? Letty, who gave only the impression of feeling dreadfully sorry for herself of late. James had behaved abominably where she was concerned, no doubt of it, but she ought really to have recovered her spirits by now. What had she meant by maintaining that Anne in her time and now Charlotte were important to James, whereas she signified nothing?

Charlotte turned from the seafarer, her talk finished. The ship's master was looking a little more human as a result of the communication, and Elizabeth was grateful. She had not found it easy, raising a new skipper and crew for the *Lady Elizabeth*. This man had looked decidedly shifty when he applied, and she had not known what to decide. But sailors in this part of the world all looked villainous, of course.

'He says he has been captaining a schooner on the Amazon, Aunt Elizabeth,' conveyed Charlotte with a smile. 'Now he has lost his command. I'm not completely clear why. He still has his crew complete, however, and they want other employment.'

'Yet does he understand steam? The *Lady Elizabeth* is something more than a schooner.'

Charlotte addressed a few more words in Portuguese to the mariner, and again he nodded vigorously, answering volubly in a tone that sounded a little contemptuous. 'Yes,' supplied Charlotte at length. 'He says he once piloted the regular steamer from Para up and down the Lower Amazon. And he has captained a coaler too, supplying other steamers. He seems a person who knows Brazil, and the area we want to go to particularly.'

It occurred yet again to Elizabeth to ask herself why she was going on this mad venture. She seemed to have been entirely swayed by Charlotte's strange fixity of purpose. What she should have done was simply take the two women back to England and leave James to his strange and wicked self-absorption. Yet she still felt that it put her at a kind of disadvantage with Daniel Fogarty if she did not try her best to rescue James from ruin. Daniel Fogarty, her husband.

Elizabeth regarded the squat ship's master before her. She supposed he was as honest as anyone else. And she really had to make up her mind. 'Very well,' she said definitively to Charlotte. 'Very well, he and his crew will do.'

Charlotte conveyed the news to the other, who at once beamed and responded with effusive gratitude, kissing Charlotte's hand a number of times. The kisses were slobbery and wet. Then he backed himself out.

'Dear me,' murmured Charlotte, rubbing her hand dry.

'It's nothing, child,' Elizabeth informed her briefly. 'Just their way.'

'But it gave me a shiver.' Charlotte was still cleansing her hand. 'Did you see his mouth, Aunt Elizabeth? Did you notice it? Such broken and rotted teeth ...'

CHAPTER SIX

When James Onedin got back to Manaos, he was all enterprise and determination. Pomaded and fulsome as ever, Senhor Lombardo tried to greet him as a long-lost brother, but James was wasting no time on any of that. 'I've left the *Neptune* at Para,' he told Baines, who was also in the dock office. 'She can be too slow in the doldrums on the river. It's better we use those *cubertas* the traders run to get the rubber upstream. Or a steamer.'

'Thought you wouldn't touch steamers,' rejoined Baines. There was an odd briskness in him. 'Thought you held they was all dirty tin kettles, good for naught else but making the tea.'

'This is business, not standing on principle,' James reminded him. 'There's still nothing to beat a white ship on the high seas, and I'll hold as much to my dying day. But we've got to achieve speed and efficiency. I docked at Bristol. Couldn't stay long, for fear those whose debts I carry heard and came too. But I reached an understanding with a merchant there. All we have to do now is keep up a supply of rubber and the money will pile up.'

'Tonight they give *Lucia di Lammermoor*,' Lombardo cut in cheerfully to inform them. They simply stared at him, and he realised with a sinking of the heart that he was stranded again among the solemn Anglo-Saxons, who doubtless would not cease from their labours even to acknowledge that so outstanding a *diva* as Sembrich had come to Manaos to sing. The opera house would one day make such appearances everyday affairs. As yet it was like a descent of the gods, to be duly hailed and recognised as such.

'Never mind all that rubbish,' snapped back James. 'We need to find out why your end of things is so disorganised.'

'Por favor, senhor? What means this?'

'According to these records,' said James, tapping a heavy ledger on the desk before him for emphasis, 'your sources are only providing you with two tons of raw rubber a fortnight. Now that's not good enough.'

'But senhor.' Lombardo spread his hands in protest and dismay. 'Consider the costs. They are so low. I have saved you much more, senhor, even than I estimated when we began our partnership.' And he reflected mournfully that in his world a man who had relieved his associate of such unnecessary expense would be entitled to put the difference into his pocket. His eyes flickered resentfully to Baines.

'Which is precisely why we must get out twice as much rubber as we're getting out now.' James was unyielding. 'You don't get rich thinking to yourself I'm buying cheap and selling dear so it means I don't need to handle so much merchandise. You get rich thinking I'm making a good profit and so I'll turn it into twice the profit by handling twice as much. I say we should set our sights on getting out at least five tons of raw rubber a fortnight.'

'Five tons! Oh, senhor – nobody has ever done this, not in the entire history of rubber. I have told you, there is not enough labour.'

'Then we'll have to find more.' A door slamming behind him told him that Baines had suddenly left the office. Something was upsetting the big seafarer, James appreciated.

Doubtless it was simply being beached too long. Well, he could get back to his sheets and halyards now. He had kept Lombardo's hand out of the till while James had been at sea, and that was sufficient. The books were in apple pie order.

'It's only a matter of applying pressure to the reliable agents up-country,' said James, sitting beside Lombardo and opening another ledger. 'This man here – Henriques or whatever his name is – he seems to be supplying you with the best regular quantity of rubber. From the region just south of Obydos. It's singularly rich. Well, we must tell him we expect him to redouble his efforts . . . '

For three quarters of an hour James sat with Lombardo, delineating business strategy. Already, with the first shipment ready to go, the profit on paper was formidable. James could see his fortune amassing even as he talked. 'Perhaps I should take decent apartments and move a little in society here,' he mused. 'The general business methods are so slack that there are probably dealers who would put all their rubber my way in return for a guarantee of efficiency. Then I could act as agent as well as exporter. All at a price, mind you. A price.'

'Ah Senhor Onedin – you will attend perhaps *Lucia di Lammermoor* tonight?' A gleam of light appeared in the universal darkness for Lombardo.

'The opera's a thing people meet at, isn't it?' James was gloomy, but saw the logic.

'All the most respected people of Manaos come. You will meet the rich, the powerful. Ah, it will be *magnifico*.' *Verranno la sull'aure . . .*

Later in the day, going down to the pontoons on some ship's business, James encountered Baines. 'See here,' he asked bluntly. 'What's the matter with you?'

'Matter with me?' rejoined Baines, leaving the question hanging. He held his bulky frame stiffly, and his voice was charged.

'Is it Lombardo? Has he sickened you with his oily ways?

89

Just stick your head over the side and get it out of your system. You'll be at sea, just you and the *Neptune* and a good crew in less than a week, with luck.'

'You want the consignment to go right away?'

'To Bristol. And I need you back as quick as can be managed for another cargo. I'm making arrangements to purchase another ship as soon as I can afford it. And a third, who knows . . .'

Toads were croaking noisily in the mud flats to the south of them. It was hard to remember sometimes that this mass of water before them was only a river. James' thoughts went yet again to Charlotte and Letty, so far away beyond the opposite bank. He supposed he missed them. He must really now write them a letter, giving his precise address. In Para, it had occurred to him that perhaps he should at least send some money in case they had run short. But that was of course a stupid scruple. Letty was an excellent manager. Excellent. Gazing downstream to where a natural channel cut through to the Rio Madeira, Baines ventured, 'These cubby-holes, or whatever tomfool name they give them – '

'*Cubertas.*'

'Well, they don't look much to me. All they've got is two masts and a forecabin. We're to trust your hard-won profit to them?'

There was an unusual sharpness in Baines' tone. 'They'll give us the fastest time upstream,' replied James, ignoring what he could not fathom. 'I estimate we'll need three. You'll pilot one, I another, and Will Brandon the third. I brought Will Brandon down with me from the *Neptune* for just that purpose.'

'Aye, I took a drink with him last night. You had it all worked out then?'

'Sound business,' commented James, still perplexed by Baines' apparent coldness towards him and what they were doing. It was as though his old companion bore him some kind of grudge. 'You need to see difficulties ahead, so that you can be prepared and overcome them.'

'Or difficulties behind,' said Baines heavily and enigmatically. 'Aye. Times are, a man needs to be awake-up to them too ...'

Daniel Fogarty waved a hand expansively about him. 'There,' he announced. 'Isn't it beautiful?'

'And this, all this is yours?'

'Every acre, as far as you can see. Right down to the water line.'

'It is beautiful,' assented Chiara Santa, dazzled by the panorama. 'Most beautiful.'

They stood on a crag where the land dropped abruptly away. A stout beam fence had been erected on the extreme edge to prevent anyone too curious from toppling over, but it was still possible to slip beneath the rail and crash to certain death below. On the lower level, wooded land ran on down to the sea. Bright sand, mile after mile of it, stretched away in an even, empty line here. All along the sunlit coast a heavy surf tumbled in.

'What will you do with it all?' asked Chiara Santa. She sounded to herself like a little girl, overawed by the magnitude of adult affairs.

'There's the timber,' answered Daniel, as though such things were of minor importance. 'There's a great deal of building going on in Sydney now. New houses, hospitals, churches, all kinds of things. And except in the city centre itself, they want to build in wood. It's finally been understood that all those stolid stone terraces in imitation of England are quite unsuited to a land like Australia.'

'Do you mean to make your life here now, Daniel? You will not go back to where you have come from?' Chiara Santa gave to the final words a curious weight. It was as though she spoke of duty, and the evasion of it. She too was an exile, overwhelmed by the beauty and generosity of a new land, at one level tempted to put down roots here, in her heart aware she flourished in a different soil. Life was unreal in these latitudes. Experience could be neither validated nor trusted.

'I think it's a great shame you have to take ship tomorrow,' said Daniel by way of reply. 'It's too soon.'

'I must go, you know that. It is my profession.'

'But you closed only last night.' Daniel had become easy with the general terminology of the theatre since seeing so much of Chiara Santa. 'Surely you should have a little holiday now. A rest.'

'No. I have accepted a booking to sing somewhere else. It is a long journey. It is my vocation.'

'Vocation?'

Chiara sighed prettily. Sometimes she did indeed feel like a missionary, called to voyage to strange lands. Everywhere the new world was opening up, and there was a voracious hunger for the culture of the old. Chiara was the nun, the votary, who could reliably bring to heathens the word of salvation. And they in no sense resisted conversion. America had fallen at her feet. Australia had worshipped at her shrine. What would happen in this next place she was ordained to visit, this outpost – ?

Daniel cut across her reflections. 'When will we meet again then? Isn't it important to know that?'

There was a strange banging in the distance, deep in the bush behind them, that might have been the thumping of a drum or a clattering of nameless metallic objects. Daniel grinned. 'I think that means luncheon is served,' he grinned.

It was a picnic, a farewell outing which Daniel had arranged for the opera company, but essentially, he was forced to admit to himself, for Chiara Santa. A specially chartered steamer had brought them all down from Sydney to the south-coast town of Helensburgh. High in the hills above the place, wrapped around by lazy warmth and the chirping of cicadas, it was possible to see the complex world for a moment blessedly remote and reduced to simplicities.

Daniel saw only that Chiara Santa was about to leave him. As of tomorrow, she would be gone. Why had Elizabeth rushed off to England like that? Simply to see to the affairs of Frazer's? It seemed the more improbable the more he thought about it. Because she had sensed a chasm between them then, and wanted space to see if it could be bridged? Weary, not of him as a person, but of the bond between them. Daniel was aware of such a chasm too. But even Elizabeth had seemed to appreciate that there was no chasm between him and Chiara Santa. Was that why she had gone?

Chiara Santa saw only that to be a missionary was to be abandoned to a life of peril. If it was not the cannibal's pot that threatened, then it was the encroachment of alien standards. Chiara did not seek to decline into pagan ways. All her life she had served the high goddess of art, and anything that did not accord with that dedication she had conscientiously put aside. Now for the first time it was more difficult. If she had loved mere men before, secular interlopers, it had been on the goddess's terms and not on theirs.

As Daniel and Chiara walked back along the bush track that had taken them to the promontory, they suddenly heard squeals of laughter and a group of young people appeared ahead. Some of the girls of the opera company were being pursued by various young men. Among these was William.

'Father!' cried William, stopping short with a gasp of laughter as he saw Daniel. 'They want you down in the meadow. They say they can't begin luncheon without you.'

'Yes, yes, William,' smiled Daniel in return. 'I'll be there in a minute. First I want to show Chiara another aspect of my property. The view from the east.'

'No, Daniel.' There had been no previous mention of anything like this, and Chiara found herself oddly perturbed. She was glad to have encountered the girls from the company. 'We can't keep everyone waiting for food.'

'Nonsense.' Daniel's smile was proprietorial. Luncheon

would be at his discretion. 'Tell them five minutes, William.'

'Yes, Father.' One of the girls abruptly plucked from William's hands a long ribbon he was clutching and dashed gleefully away. William blinked about him, bewildered, and the youthful company hooted with laughter. William at once set off after the girl. It was some game they were playing. Daniel led Chiara in another direction, his strong hand guiding her purposefully.

'Daniel.' Chiara had become unaccustomedly nervous. She could not tell why. 'It is impolite of you not to go to the meadow at once. Your guests will be hungry. The open air gives a good appetite.'

'I don't want you to go tomorrow,' returned Daniel, propelling her along. 'Whatever this engagement you've taken elsewhere in the world, call it off. I'll see to any financial loss.'

'No. It is not possible. It is in South America.'

'South America?'

'A city in the jungle where they love opera. And then afterwards I have to go to Rio de Janeiro. I must keep faith. It is a part of my work.'

'I've hardly thought about my work lately,' Daniel informed her. 'Do you know that? Any time I try and concentrate on it, your face rises up before me. It's no good, Chiara. The simple fact is, you and I –'

'Stop this!' Chiara pulled her arm away from Daniel. It was too much. She had, after all, taken the veil. Secular interlopers could take impermissible liberties. 'I don't know what you can be thinking of. These are most improper notions for you to be entertaining. We will now go to luncheon, please.'

'Will you stay on tomorrow?'

'No.'

'Chiara . . . Chiara, my love. You must! Don't you see – you've no choice?'

It was very still where they had stopped. The tiniest breeze

94

stirred the bush about, and sunlight filtered down through the trees, dappling their faces. The cicadas, the picnic party, the world were very far away. Daniel put a gentle arm round Chiara's waist, pulling her closer to him. She found that she had no power to object. Not of her own volition, her hands went up around his neck.

Daniel's lips pressed hard on hers. It occurred to Chiara in some impotent part of her mind that of course something should have been said about his wife. On her tamer and better cultivated soil that matter would at least have been discussed. But a nun taken unawares is no doubt not entitled to such niceties. She felt extraordinarily like Leonora in Act Two of *Il Trovatore*. The familiar notes of the great aria soared up inside her. But unaccountably, they had the resonances of the *Miserere*.

Chiara, so used to the eyes of the world upon her, would not have thought at this moment to have an audience. Daniel would have been alarmed to suspect he was being spied upon. But concealed in a clump of scrub not far from them, William watched and William noted.

William knew now he had been right to come secretly after his father rather than go to the meadow as he had been requested. He had suspected something of this sort for a long time. His father's affections had clearly strayed, after he had solemnly assured his son there was no possibility of it.

Suddenly William was angry. All his thoughts went to his mother, and he conceived the rapid notion that he should be at her side. At such a time his place was surely not in this land which she had never liked, which she had rejected, but where she was, supporting his abused, neglected, sadly betrayed mother.

The wind took the mainsail quite without warning, and spun the *cuberta* round in the water like a top. 'Lord above,' gasped Baines, grabbing at the forecabin as he was hurled heavily back against it. 'She's naught but a damned match-box.'

'Trovoada de cima,' howled one of his hands behind him, jabbing a finger upstream.

'Which – ?' yelled Baines.

'Trovoada de cima.'

Baines' talent for picking up the meaning of what sea-farers said, never mind the language they saw fit to use, had for some reason or other deserted him on this particular trip downriver to Para. Perhaps it was because he had no genuine sympathy with the hands, who were basically land-lubbers, and heartily disliked the *cuberta*. It was impossible to love such a craft as a man loved a real ship. She was little more than a glorified barge. For deepwater sailors such as Baines, the final and bitter fate was to end up a bargee.

The provision was that the rubber, the collection of which Lombardo had arranged while James had been at sea, was to be brought to a series of river landings. (Baines could not dignify some of them with the name of ports.) The *cubertas*, travelling independently but staying as close together as pos-sible, would call into each of these in rotation, thus ensuring even spread of the cargo as a whole until they reached the *Neptune*, where all would be transferred. They were just coming up to the landing south of Obydos where the biggest load of all was to be taken aboard, so all three craft would put in here.

Another yell rent the air. Baines glanced behind him. The *cuberta* James was piloting was just aft of him, and James was on the prow, pointing upstream and shouting something. Baines shaded his eyes and peered ahead. He perceived in a second that *trovoada de cima* must be some local term for a river storm. A belt of driving rain was fast approaching them, whirled along at a spanking rate by a stiff wind. As the storm hit the river banks, the high trees, a moment ago tall and still sentinels, began to toss and sway alarmingly.

As the rain lashed down on them, hard and stinging as

pellets, a sudden wave raised by the wind struck the bows and jolted the *cuberta* violently, again swinging it round.

'Shorten sail,' yelled Baines. 'Get her in close as you can and tie up. We're near enough to the damned landing anyway. Time to lay to.'

Baines navigated the *cuberta* out of the mainstream and into the shallows. Some wading birds in the mud reaches screeched at them, confused by the speed and violence of the storm. Drenched to the skin and thoroughly fed up, Baines got a line ashore and sent a hand after it to secure and made his way back to the forecabin, where he sat down to a pensive pipe.

The sooner he was finished with all this, he reflected as the rain pelted down, the happier he would be. River pilots had always struck him as an odd lot, and now he knew why. You could pile up on a sandbank right out in stream if you weren't careful sometimes. When you hove-to at night you had to lie on a great length of cable so that you wouldn't be close enough in for the damned mosquitoes to eat you alive. Then there were the ticks that burrowed into you. You had to spend at least an hour a night picking them out of your body. Other things in this whole damned business fretted you too. Other things.

Once the storm had passed, James came up alongside Baines, as did Will Brandon in his *cuberta*. James tied up and came aboard Baines' craft. 'Henriques isn't here yet,' he observed. 'But he'll be along before sunset. He's a good man. Knows we're due this afternoon.'

'Who's Henriques?' asked Baines bluntly.

'Agent in these parts. He's done well, according to the books.'

'Ah. Clever devil who got the biggest haul of rubber, you mean.' Baines gave a hard smile. 'Aye. I mind him. Enterprising cully, I'd say.'

James frowned. The grudging note was evident once more. 'Are you going to tell me what's biting you besides horseflies,' he asked the big seafarer weightily, 'or is it to remain a mystery till the seas dry up?'

Baines glowered at the tangle of green on the bank against which he was moored. He wondered about bats and he wondered about snakes. The sea proper might be a hard life, but there were things a man would not have to endure there. At sea a man was properly free. That was the real distinction, Baines thought bleakly: ashore: incarceration, disease, wild animals and slavery: at sea: liberty.

'I'll tell you this much,' said Baines in reply to James. 'There's a difference between mutton stew and a sheep found dead in a swamp.' Now the response was not only enigmatic but downright obscure. Baines was not a man who chose always to give expression to his thoughts.

Henriques arrived after they had been at the landing place about an hour. He brought five donkey carts with him, each of them loaded with raw rubber. The stuff was of a dark and spongey consistency. It was the liquid tapped out of the rubber trees, congealed and then coagulated into masses. Silent Indians drove the carts and Henriques was mounted on a tall black horse. He was a stringy but muscular man, obviously respected by those who served him.

'Splendid . . . splendid!' James gloated over the quantity of rubber, mightily pleased. 'How often can you let me have rubber in this sort of bulk?'

Henriques waved a hand at the forest behind him. 'You say, Capitao,' he returned in broken English. 'Everywhere rubber trees. You say how much I get.'

'But it's a question of how much you can manage at a time. Your workers.'

'Plenty workers.' Again Henriques waved a hand, this time at the Indians. 'Plenty good workers. Plenty *Muras*.'

'*Muras* –'

'Indian peoples. Many live in jungle. They work for Henriques.' And he flashed a dazzling grin at the Indians in the carts. They returned his cheerful smile. But it was

98

like oil lamps going on, it struck James: one face lighting up after the other, quickly suffused with a bland, stark glow.

'I'll take every ounce you can provide,' James told him. 'Every ounce.' He had a sudden vision of the future, gem-encrusted now, far richer even than he had dreamed. This section of Brazil alone was far larger than Europe. Rubber trees had been growing here for thousands of years. There was arguably no end to the money he could make, the trade he could found and expand.

The rubber was loaded and secured aboard the *cubertas*, and Henriques and the Indians left. The Portuguese cracked a long whip above their heads, doubtless to encourage the donkeys. James searched out Baines, who had not been in evidence any more than necessary since the arrival of the trader.

'I think we'll lay to overnight,' he said. 'Cast off at first light.'

'Aye, aye, Cap'n.' Baines chose to be formal and snapped a smart salute.

James was irritated. 'Damn your eyes, man,' he expostulated, 'what *is* it you fret about?'

'Is it the same free crew as ever aboard the *Neptune* when we reach her,' Baines demanded to know, 'or some filthy press gang?'

'What are you talking about?'

'You heard him then, did you?' Baines looked sharply to James, his eyes alight. Night was coming down and his glance was a bright spark in the shadows. 'Your grand Senhor Henriques. Plenty of workers in the jungle. Plenty of *Muras*.'

'He gets his labour where he can. He must. The Indians will work for wages after all. Lombardo was in error.'

'Wages!' Baines scoffed and spat over the side into the water. 'You think that clever devil pays those poor naturals wages?'

'What else would he do?' James' voice was rising.

'What else! My God, Captain Onedin, sir, you're a contrary party.' Now Baines' eyes flashed in the gloom. 'You'd lead me and half a good crew into danger to relieve the master of a schooner of his human cargo, and yet you'd settle back and reap every penny profit you could out of the slaving of a villain like that!'

'Slaving? What makes you say he's slaving?' James heard his own voice echo back at him from the trees. The jungle was an empty cathedral when the shades drew in. The incessant chatter of the birds and monkeys stopped, and the mighty trunks were sounding ribs and arches.

'Not a penny on the books this one sets down for wages. Didn't your confab with Senhor Lombardo show you that?'

'Lombardo explained. Henriques likes to be paid in a lump sum. Then he can simply move about as he has to, contract labour wherever he finds the need. Naturally he can't make a proper return of what he pays out on wages.'

'Which all helps him get the biggest quantity of rubber cheapest – ?'

'Perhaps. I don't know the ins and outs of it. I simply look to my profit . . . ' The echo rang irony back to him. Baines was an almost invisible lump before him now. James scoffed. 'Sometimes, Mr Baines, you don't know what you're complaining about.' James was the captain on the bridge all at once, concerned to put an obstreperous mate in his place. 'Slavery is outlawed in this country, and there are heavy penalties against it. If Senhor Henriques is using slave labour, then he'll pay the price for it sooner or later. Don't you worry about that. But until he does, it's no concern of mine. No concern of mine!'

James swung himself ashore from the *cuberta*, turning for his own vessel where already a light gleamed. 'Ruin,' he spat back into the darkness. 'Do you know the meaning of ruin? To have risked all on a venture that could benefit thousands, then to have lost all through a quirk of fortune. There's men couldn't take that. Men who'd die. Or kill themselves. But James Onedin isn't of that ilk.' The voice was firm, incisive. It cut across the night. 'I've seen to my wife and child as best I may, but even their needs come second to what I have to do here and now. So I'll look to my own affairs, Mr Baines, and leave others to look to theirs. We none of us need telling it's an evil world. But you gather in no harvest moaning about that. You reap no profit lamenting human wickedness.'

CHAPTER SEVEN

Baines felt more himself again once a stout deck rose and fell under his feet and the wind cracked out the broad expanse of the main course. Looking aloft as the *Neptune* sped along, he wondered if the divines were not right to talk of the Lord walking on the wings of the wind. Baines was an indifferent churchgoer, but he had before today encountered the divinity in the shrouds. Existence was clean and pure up there on the shuddering yards, and no evil could encroach. Smoke stacks concealed no eternal truths, however. Steam was irreligious and the coal boiler atheist.

James Onedin took Baines' *cuberta* in tow, and he and Will Brandon piloted their crafts back to Manaos. They did not travel empty and profitless. Some fashioned marble had been shipped to Para from Carara in Italy. It was for a section of the Manaos Opera House which was soon to rise from the unsuspecting river bank. James shipped it willingly. It would consolidate his position with those wealthy merchants who already saw him as a 'coming' man, and the creation of the Teatro Amazonas as the culmination of consecrated dreams and ambitions.

When he arrived back at Manaos, James found a letter waiting for him. The handwriting was Letty's. James at once opened it, for he had finally despatched a missive to Sao Paulo and took it this was Letty's dutiful reply, outlining how she was managing. But the contents confused and shocked him. *My dear James,* the flowing yet cramped script read, *I cannot conceive why you are behaving as you are. Even Elizabeth is at a loss to know. Yes, your sister Elizabeth. She has come to this country, found us, and is appalled at our condition. If Charlotte had not in the main recovered from her injuries . . .*

The letter ran on over several pages, the handwriting becoming more disjointed and less regular as it progressed. Letty had spent her days as a governess instilling into her various young charges the necessity of always corresponding in copperplate, so it must have come to something if she could let her own writing go in such a fashion. Yet what was the matter precisely? The letter read as though there had been others preceding it. James noticed for the first time that the envelope was addressed simply *Captain James Onedin, Manaos.* It was as though she were shouting at him. James recalled that Letty had shouted at him once before – on the night of the tempest in Port Baines, when he had had for the first time to face the disturbing fact that he did not truly care for her, and the perhaps more disturbing fact that she was jealous of Charlotte.

Elizabeth says that for you to have left us unprovided in this fashion . . . Elizabeth! Now what on earth was Elizabeth doing in Brazil? James had supposed her to be still in Australia with her husband. It was bewildering and a little outrageous. *Unprovided* was into the bargain a gross exaggeration. James had been deeply concerned lest there should be inconvenience and had weighed the matter up many times in his mind with great seriousness, but was not Letty's management of affairs to be called into question before there was complaint of his neglect? He had provided as he had supposed, very well, and if he had not in the event assured himself that all was as it should be, it had been because of his dedication to a solution to the large problems.

The letter ended with a bombshell. '... *and so we have decided to come in search of you in your city of Manaos. There you will be able to make up to us for the humiliation we have suffered. Extraordinarily enough, Charlotte still believes it is her duty to "help" you. For my part* ...'

James put the missive away from him in sudden anger. He allowed that with the best will in the world, he might conceivably have been a little remiss. He really had very little true idea of domestic costs. Charlotte at least seemed to hold nothing against him. If anything she apparently wanted to aid him in his struggle. Well, that was generous affection, the kind that was needed in a family. But Elizabeth. Oh, why was Elizabeth in Brazil? What did it purport...?

'He doesn't love me,' declared Letty solemnly. 'He never did ...'

Opposite her, Elizabeth stirred uneasily. They were in the master's cabin and day room of the *Lady Elizabeth*, which they had converted to a little suite for themselves and Charlotte. The squat captain whom Elizabeth had hired (whose name turned out to be Furtado) had been given other quarters, and he and his crew were not much in evidence in the normal way. Furtado himself made a daily report to Elizabeth, and there was a negro who brought them their meals. Otherwise they were left alone as the ship made steady headway up the long coast of Brazil. They were still at sea, but soon would alter course to enter the mouth of the Amazon. Elizabeth was glad of that, for the bucketing of the tramp combined with the constant vibration of her engines still made her feel a little sick. Letty's constant complaining of course did nothing to improve her health.

'I'm sure you're going too far, saying that,' Elizabeth sighed as she seemed to have sighed so many times before.

The absurd thing was she was being forced to defend James in order to have a hope of halting Letty's flow. 'James is under a terrible strain just now. He hasn't time for the usual displays of affection.'

'He never had,' insisted Letty. 'He began by informing me when I was a governess that I was to marry him. It was abrupt, quite alarming. When I refused his terms, he seemed perplexed. Then after much thought, he took me on a romantic cruise of the Scottish isles. He seemed to imagine that it would soften my resolve. It did,' confessed Letty, again very solemn. 'It did.'

Elizabeth remembered a romantic cruise too. Aboard the *Neptune,* which she had heard was the only brigantine James had managed to save from disaster, with dear old Baines at the helm, and her brand new husband at her side. Daniel Fogarty. She still saw his handsome face gazing keenly out to sea as the mizzen bellied above them and the boom swung slowly round like a mighty branch. But did he love her? Had he ever? Men, Elizabeth reflected, were to be compared to the clipper ships of former days. Noble, inviting fulsome trust and confidence, but once at sea concerned only to put on all sail for the next port of call. It was supposed to be healthy for trade. Elizabeth smiled wryly. The face of Chiara Santa came unbidden into her mind. Really, she thought, if Letty were not so perpetually long-faced, the two of them might have had a good deal to talk about. But then it was impossible to talk properly to Letty. It was necessary to stay at a distance from her in order to keep the peace between her and Charlotte.

It was extraordinary how all that had begun. It had taken Elizabeth quite unawares. From Santos they had gone on to Rio de Janeiro, where Charlotte had begged to be allowed ashore. Furtado for his part was against docking at Rio. It seemed to be something to do with the schooner he had lost, and his crew supported him in opposing a landfall. The capital appeared to hold bad memories for all of them.

Charlotte had pleaded with Elizabeth, because the final decision as to whether the *Lady Elizabeth* put in at Rio or not was obviously hers.

'Please, Aunt Elizabeth,' begged the girl earnestly. 'I may never be here again. Look at the Sugar Loaf there. Wouldn't it be splendid to see it more closely? And I hear the Guanabara Palace is an architectural gem, which it would advance my education to study. And who knows – since she lives there, I might even encounter the Princess Izabel.'

'Stuff and nonsense, girl,' Letty had cut in. They were standing on the foredeck as the ship lay in stream, gazing towards the city. A bright sun beat down on them. It seemed without doubt the sort of day for an excursion. 'You can read about things to advance your education. You don't wish to go ashore for any serious purpose at all. Merely to wear your finest clothes and parade the streets, hoping to catch the eye of some unsuspecting passer-by.'

'Letty.' Charlotte was surprised by the attack, as was Elizabeth. She knew her niece to be a normal young woman, but did not think her consumed by vanity or a flirt. 'Truly I wish to see Rio de Janeiro. It is one of the greatest cities of all South America. I will effect a compromise,' said Charlotte with a sudden smile, for she liked to make little jokes and was generally successful with them. 'I will wear a blindfold and my oldest clothes if you think my motives less than pure, so that the populace will take me for nothing but a poor beggar woman. And I will lift the veil only when some kind nun or charitable person assures me that I am standing in front of Our Lady of Candelaria.'

Elizabeth laughed, but Letty's face froze into a hard mask. 'Kindly do not be frivolous,' she snapped. 'It really is of very little consequence to me whether you go on this jaunt ashore or not. I am merely anxious as your guardian that you should not deceive yourself about your true reasons for wishing to undertake it.'

'Letty,' remonstrated Elizabeth. 'She's young. It's nothing more than that.'

'Nothing more?' Now an odd shrillness had entered Letty's tone. 'Nothing more? I trust I am a better judge of the child's character than you, Elizabeth. After all, I have had to stand sentinel over it for many years now, whereas you come to it quite inexperienced. You are vulnerable where I am resistant.'

'Inexperienced – ?' Elizabeth was entirely baffled as to what Letty might be saying.

'She is young, you suggest. Subject to enthusiasms.' The words came cracking out, not particularly loudly since Letty would not have wished to attract the attention of any of the crew who were in the vicinity. But they had unmistakable force and bite. 'She first persuaded you to turn over your ship to our needs so that she might hasten to her harassed father's side. It was very moving, was it not? Most touching?'

'Please,' cried Charlotte, a beginning of tears in her eyes. 'What is it you wish of me?'

'But now we see the true reason for that sentimental plea. It was simply and solely to arrange for herself a pleasure cruise. Something entirely selfish. A carefree trip, in the course of which she might visit romantic places and even while aboard, be the centre of attention.'

'Stop this,' demanded Elizabeth, beginning not to like what was happening at all.

'Have you noticed the way she behaves with the crew?' There was obviously no stopping Letty now. 'This – riffraff that no decent girl should do more than acknowledge?'

Charlotte bit her lip and quickly looked out to sea. She had begun to cry.

'I speak only for your own good, child,' continued Letty in a lower and less impassioned tone. The tears were 'first blood', and she apparently at once decided to be accommodating. 'To fulfil my duty to you and your father. You must at length try to understand your own deficiencies. You think because you have mastered a little of the crew's tongue that that permits you at almost any time to run and chatter to them. But it's a grave mistake, my dear. You'd love to have men at your feet, of course, the whole world adoring you. Few young women of your disposition wouldn't. But there are plenty of unfortunates to tell you how that sort of ambition turns out.'

Letty patted her bun of hair. Charlotte turned and ran for the quarters they all shared, in the circumstances the only place she could hope to be alone. Elizabeth was quite astonished. 'Letty,' she asked in some confusion. 'What on earth was all that about?'

'Charlotte knows. There are no mysteries between Charlotte and myself.'

'But you made her cry.'

'Tears have been her defence ever since she was very young. Charlotte knows. Charlotte knows,' Letty repeated coldly.

Plainly, there was to be no excursion into the town that day. The *Lady Elizabeth* raised anchor and proceeded on her way, much to the gratification of Furtado. In fact he was almost too grateful, and thanked Elizabeth in such a torrent of Portuguese that she found it suspicious. There was some good reason why Furtado and his crew had not wanted the *Lady Elizabeth* to delay at Rio. Had his schooner been halted there? Seized from him? Yet by whom? And why? Elizabeth knew Rio to be a well policed city and port.

Later that same day when she went back to their quarters, Elizabeth was surprised to find the cabin in which the three women slept locked from the outside. She at once opened it. Charlotte sat within on a bunk, dismal and preoccupied.

'Charlotte,' frowned Elizabeth. 'What does this mean?'

'Letty locked me in,' replied the girl in some shame.

Angered, Elizabeth went in search of her sister-in-law. It was obvious that her years as a governess had left her with some notions of discipline that would be better forgotten. She found Letty on the deck aft, seated out of the sun with a book.

'She's not a baby any more, Letty,' Elizabeth pointed out stiffly. 'Anyway I'm not sure I ever cared for the practice of locking children in rooms or even cupboards because they'd been naughty. Aboard ship it's positively dangerous. What if there were an alarm?'

'Aboard a ship like this?' enquired Letty drily, her eyes taking in the still bright paint and barely trodden timbers of the *Lady Elizabeth.* 'On her maiden voyage? I should have thought you would have had more confidence in your own shipyards. But as to Charlotte,' said her stepmother, settling more comfortably back into the chair she occupied, 'whenever she decides to behave in a reasonable and adult fashion, she will find me perfectly amenable. I do not intend to spoonfeed her. Charlotte is wilful, selfish and deliberately immature. I cannot reasonably object if James prefers her to me, Elizabeth. She is his daughter. His and Anne's. But I do feel he should be apprised of the truth about her at last. The truth . . .'

So from that time forward, Elizabeth sought to obviate strife and become an angel of peace between Letty Onedin and her stepdaughter.

It was not until they reached Para at the mouth of the Amazon that the tension which Letty had allowed to build up between herself and Charlotte abated, and then only because other preoccupations supervened. Letty was feeling ill at Para and would not go ashore, so Elizabeth took Charlotte into the town with her, and together they had a wonderful day. The mixed racial character of the colourful river port enchanted Charlotte and re-awakened her interest in the native peoples of Brazil.

'The Indians come and go in Para perfectly freely,'

chattered Charlotte excitedly, indicating what seemed at a glance a hundred or more canoes, all secured like toys before the vast wall of the jungle. 'That friar I spoke to told me. They trade all kinds of things. The native language in these parts is the dialect called Tupi-Guarani. But that doesn't mean there aren't local languages as well. Everybody has to speak about three of them at least.'

'Goodness, what a great deal you know, Charlotte dear,' smiled Elizabeth, happy for her youthful involvement. She wondered idly if it was the girl's youth and beauty, and simply that, that Letty resented.

'I want to know more, Aunt Elizabeth. Much more. Papa's interests are now almost entirely in this land – isn't that so?'

'You don't imagine he'll stay here?'

'I hope he gets out of his difficulties,' responded Charlotte seriously. 'And I hope he understands at long last just how much Letty has given to him. That's the worst part of this – neglect of his, if you can call it that. Letty feels it's all directed at her.'

Furtado took on the largest possible consignment of coal at Para, which Elizabeth supposed was wise. The supply ships which plied between these parts and the North American seaboard would doubtless have only minimal stocks further down the Amazon. The *Lady Elizabeth* circumnavigated Marajo Island in leisurely fashion and entered the mainstream. Charlotte was altogether occupied with her study of tongues and customs, and Letty was self-absorbed. Overcast days followed by moonless nights came down on them as they passed through the barren Dry Campos region.

One night when she seemed only to have been sleeping for an hour, Elizabeth was awakened by a frightened scream. She thought herself dreaming, then perceived Charlotte just across from her, thrust back against the bulkhead and terrified. A guttering lantern held by a crewman

110

gave light, and Letty was on her feet, shouting at Furtado and two other members of the crew who were also there. Both the women were in their nightdresses.

'Get out!' a near-hysterical Letty was screeching at the intruders. 'How dare you! Get out!'

'What is this? Captain Furtado . . . ' Still only half-awake, Elizabeth tumbled out of her bunk, grabbing a dressing gown and throwing it around her shoulders.

Furtado swung dull eyes on Elizabeth. His expression was surly and unpleasant. Used to a kind of canine subservience from him, Elizabeth was alarmed. She got the immediate impression that he had been drinking. 'You are not permitted to enter this cabin,' she told him with as much hauteur as she could muster. 'Kindly leave at once. Your behaviour is outrageous, and we shall speak about it in the morning.'

'They mean to kill us,' shouted Letty. 'Kill us!' And she burst into frightened tears.

'Letty, kindly don't be ridiculous.' Elizabeth was not quite as sanguine as she sounded, but found strength in the reflection that after all this was only a matter of dealing with drunken men, just as in Liverpool. For all the crew members present were plainly intoxicated. One man swayed so visibly that it seemed certain he must fall. 'You may go, Captain Furtado.'

'No go,' answered the squat Portuguese in slurred tones. 'No go. You go.'

Elizabeth was taken aback, for she had not until that moment thought the little man to have a single word of English. What was more he was being insolent, which did not accord with their previous relationship. 'We're lost, Aunt Elizabeth.' It was Charlotte's voice from the bulkhead, shaky yet bravely contained. 'I said something to him in Portuguese. He means to –'

With a scowl, Furtado spat on to the timbers and took a step towards Charlotte. He raised a hand to her. Elizabeth did not pause an instant, but quickly thrust herself between him and the fearful girl. 'No!' she rapped. 'No, don't touch this child! Get out! I'll have you jailed for this. Jailed, do you hear me? Leave us alone or it will be the worse for you. This is my ship.'

'Ship,' muttered Furtado. He glared at Elizabeth, then shook his head blearily. 'Your ship. No your ship. Furtado, he one time have ship. Fine ship. Government man, he take ship while Furtado in Rio. Furtado now cannot get back ship. So he have your ship. Your ship.'

'It's what I was trying to tell you, Aunt Elizabeth,' cried Charlotte. She was holding back tears only by a supreme effort. 'They want to take over the ship.'

'Mutiny!' Elizabeth was appalled. She had only heard of such things. Her eyes were furious as they flashed to Furtado again. 'You're being altogether stupid. They could hang you for such a thing. Put you to death! Don't you understand? Are you serious? Why did the Brazilian government impound your ship in Rio? Are you a criminal?'

Furtado made no reply for a moment, then slowly grinned. His breath was foul, wafting into Elizabeth's face out of the broken and rotted teeth. He looked drunkenly to Charlotte. He paused a long moment, then once more raised his hand. It moved uncertainly in the direction of the girl's shoulder and hovered over the sleeve of her nightdress. It came to Elizabeth with a shock that the little Portuguese had perhaps not meant to strike her when he raised his hand to her before. He had humiliation of another sort in mind. 'Get out!' she screamed, suddenly angered in a new way. Her stomach heaved and she felt ill. She faced her oppressor courageously. She knew that if her stomach rebelled, she would vomit right in his face.

Furtado paused. Some of her intense outrage and contempt obviously reached him, for he looked for a moment crestfallen, again like a dog that had disgraced itself. Then his face set in a hard line. 'English peoples,' he spat. 'Furtado hate English peoples. English captain, one time he steal from Furtado. Steal cargo . . . ' He swung once more on Charlotte and barked something at her in Portuguese. Then he spat on the floor again and jerked an order at the crewmen. He lurched out of the cabin, the others on his heels. The hatch was pulled hard to and locked from the outside.

A complete silence followed. Even Letty's sobbing had ceased. 'We're to get dressed,' said Charlotte in a dead voice. 'He's taking the ship from us, Aunt Elizabeth. He means . . . he means to put us ashore.'

The night was darker than ever as the ship's boat, lowered while they were dressing, took Elizabeth, Letty and Charlotte towards the river bank. There was no sound apart from the creak of the rowlocks. It seemed an outlandish turn of events. From being unable to believe any of it was actually happening, Elizabeth had tried desperately to turn her mind to the question of what to take with her. It was impossible to say what kind of terrain they would be abandoned in, or for how long. Impossible to say if there was even any point in thinking of survival as a serious option: would Furtado leave them food? Elizabeth had been helped in choosing various implements, selecting clothing, by a surprisingly calm Charlotte. 'We must take a comb,' Elizabeth remembered she had said with detached practicality. 'A good strong comb.'

A gentle sound of sobbing told her that Letty had broken down again. Three large men were conveying them the considerable distance from the ship to the river bank. 'Stop that, Letty,' said Elizabeth shortly, hoping she sounded at least as calm as Charlotte had done. Where had the girl found the resources? 'Don't give them the satisfaction. We'll be all right.'

It was probably the stupidest assurance she had ever given. She could not tell what on earth was going to happen to them. She wondered fretfully why Furtado, if disposing of them was what he had in mind, had not simply killed them and left it at that. She supposed that until he was out of Amazonian waters with his stolen ship, the corpse of the owner and her two close relatives could prove an embarrassment to him. He meant to head for the open sea, obviously. He had taken on so much coal at Para to make a long journey possible.

A strange croaking was heard. It took a moment to realise it was frogs, and that they were finally approaching the river bank. One of the seamen shone a lantern ahead, illuminating the way into the shallows. The other men shipped oars, and after a little the boat ran gently up on to the mud, lurching to a stop.

Elizabeth, Letty and Charlotte were bundled ashore like cattle, stumbling and slithering in the mud. The boat pushed away without a word from the seamen, and vanished in silence.

'They've murdered us,' sobbed Letty. 'As sure as if they'd taken a knife and run it into us. They've murdered us.'

'Listen to the jungle,' said Charlotte in gentle tones. 'Listen . . . ' As well as the frogs, there was a sound of insects: subdued, but persistent as a ground bass. If you strained your ears, you could hear birds: owls, night jars, stretching away into the distance in endless chorus. And the foliage moved incessantly. It was plain that the jungle, nourished by the river, teemed with life. Aware for the first time of what they might be abandoned to, Elizabeth shivered with apprehension, and wished she could see Charlotte's face.

CHAPTER EIGHT

'But where has he gone?' queried Chiara Santa in puzzled tones. 'Forgive me, Daniel caro, but I do not understand.'

She had taken to addressing him more familiarly, which he supposed was a good thing. Yet the fact was, he reminded himself glumly, that nothing had occurred to justify her use of such endearments. Chiara had not in the event left Sydney with the rest of the opera company. They had returned to their native Italy, and Chiara had on impulse despatched an international cable to a man in the United States who ordered her professional affairs saying that 'illness and exhaustion' prevented her proceeding at once to her engagement in Brazil. Then she had departed on a tour of his New South Wales properties with Daniel. This tour had been most respectably conducted, Chiara at each stopping place insisting on sharing quarters with her maid. Lady Elizabeth, she had remarked more than once, would expect that.

Daniel stared at the letter in his hand. He had already decided he was mystified by Chiara Santa's attitude. He had found her propriety on the tour coy, to say the least. She was a woman of the world, and must surely have known what interpretation he placed on her decision to stay on with him rather than go at once to South America. It was ended with

115

Elizabeth. Ended. He saw that quite clearly now. He had had no word from her save the formal notification of her arrival in England. She was plainly rejoiced to be relieved of his presence.

'William says in this letter he's gone to join his mother,' said Daniel, puzzled himself. 'He has money of his own, you know. He can do as he pleases. So he has left for England.'

'When, Daniel?'

'The letter is dated a month ago. He would be nearing the end of his voyage by now. We were away a long time, Chiara.' And he remembered how he had deliberately extended the tour, in the ever paler hope that something would happen to break down Chiara's reserve. It became more and more perplexing. There had been a moment of romance, under a jewelled night high in the Blue Mountains, when they had embraced again. But Chiara had subtly indicated that she should not have permitted that to happen. What had occurred? Had Chiara repented of her earlier attraction to him? Did she find herself repelled by him after all?

'Why should William wish to go and join his mother?' enquired Chiara, thinking of her holy dedication, her vows to the goddess, and how she had for a mad moment been tempted to play fast and loose with them. 'Does he miss her so dreadfully?'

'I don't know.' It was hardly a question of morals, surely. A woman like Chiara Santa would not be constrained in that way. It was ended with Elizabeth. She must have known it. 'Frankly I'm only concerned that he may have misunderstood my wishes for him.'

'Why should he? You are generous towards him, a good father.' She was attracted to Daniel Fogarty, yes. He was an exciting man. But his love would be demanding, and such a demand would conflict with the demands on her of her religion, which remained her art.

'Also, he may not like my – ways.' Daniel was not so stupid as to suppose William's departure entirely uncon-

116

nected with his interest in Chiara Santa. The boy had as good as accused him of too much involvement with the opera singer. 'My intention was to place choices before him. All the choices this new land offers. Yet he may have taken it for indifference. Through no fault of mine, you see, he spent a great deal of his life without a knowledge of my concern for him.'

'Poor Daniel.' Chiara felt truly sorry for him. But if she allowed herself to love Daniel, she would end by serving him. It was the way of such loves. And if she served Daniel Fogarty, that would be an end of her service to the high goddess. Love and art were irreconcilables. Had not the fickle Philina discovered so to her cost in *Mignon*? 'I have enjoyed our time together. I am grateful to you for persuading me to stay and have a holiday. But now, finally, I must go to South America.'

'Chiara,' said Daniel suddenly. They were in the great living room of his house in Balmain. It was not necessarily the end yet. 'Please. Tell me why –'

'No, Daniel caro.' Her voice was loud and commanding in the big room. It was a voice that had filled theatres and reduced great orchestras to the merest accompaniment. It was the voice the goddess had bestowed on her. 'I am most truly grateful to you. I will never forget all you have done for me. But now I must return to my profession. It is my life. Without it . . . I do not exist.'

'Well, where is the rubber?' asked James angrily. 'Why was it held up?'

Little Lombardo shrugged expansively. It was his standard reaction now to the bristling responses of this dour Anglo-Saxon with whom he was unfortunately in business. He had come seriously to wonder if the English had been supplied with souls at their creation. At the *musicale* the other evening (they were being held regularly in the government salons these days to help finance the opera house) Captain Onedin had shifted and fidgeted all through selections from *Il Barbiere di Siviglia*, anxious only for the interval when he might give himself once more to business contacts and the pursuit of wealth. And Sembrich herself there to sing Rosina!

'Senhor Onedin,' pointed out Lombardo as reasonably as he could, 'we cannot tell. But Senhor Henriques was not at the landing place with the agreed consignment of rubber when Captain Baines arrived to collect it.'

'Why, Baines?'

James switched his irritated gaze to the big seafarer. They stood on the poop of the *Neptune*, which should by rights not have been in Manaos at all, but which Baines had brought upstream. 'What the devil do you think you're doing?' James had snapped at Baines, leaping aboard the vessel as she docked and the plank came down. 'You're not supposed to bring the *Neptune* beyond Para. I've five *cubertas* on the river at this moment, proceeding to supply her.'

'They'll be laying to, then. Heavy weather downstream. Better I came here, got your instructions.'

'Dammit, man, you had instructions. Perfectly clear instructions.' James had wondered what could be wrong with the fellow. 'Don't you believe in obeying orders? The time you've wasted, coming back to Manaos! You're losing me money!'

'I'd remind you I'm lawful master of the *Neptune*, Captain Onedin, sir.' Baines had been very stiff all at once, setting his jaw and drawing himself up to his prodigious height. 'I make all dispositions in her regard. And I'll not swap a fine brig for a filthy river cubbyhole just to suit your purposes, sir. You're making money enough out of this venture. There's poor devils aren't, I daresay, but you're right as a trivet. If such money as you make in this caper can ever be called right.'

It was as frank as Baines had been. For his part, James had closed his mind to the whole question of how rubber was procured on his behalf, and by what species of labour. He himself would never willingly consent to the use of slaves, obviously. That would be cruel and unprincipled. But what others did in this vast land of conflicting customs and moral standards was their own business. Come to that, had anybody actually produced hard evidence to say Henriques *was* employing slave labour?

James had let the matter go at that, and sent Baines and the *Neptune* to pick up the rubber from the *cubertas* at the specified landing places. Now Baines was back again to say there had been no consignment as expected at the landing south of Obydos. James glared at him. It smacked again of a deliberate waste of time. 'Why wasn't Henriques at the landing place with his rubber, I asked?'

Baines again set his jaw and held himself erect. A little wind above them played in the reefed shrouds, singing a plaintive song. 'Well, Captain Onedin,' answered the mariner in crisp tones, 'that's the mystery of all the world. I laid off overnight and waited, but he didn't come the next morning either. So I went ashore with four of the lads. A couple of miles inland there's a house of sorts. Nothing to write home about – just lathe and mud, stuck in a clearing. Yet it had all these rush mats spread around it, and stakes druv in the ground. Stakes with chains attached.'

'This is the house of Senhor Henriques,' nodded Lombardo. 'I have been there.'

'Then perhaps you could tell me what it is he keeps chained to them stakes as a regular thing, sir,' continued Baines, shooting a hard glance in the Italian's direction. 'I thought it must be goats as he didn't want to stray, but then it came to me there's few keeps goats in these parts. It's the mystery of the world again, for whatever it is he had there is gone. Vanished into thin air with Henriques himself. And that made the Brazilian gentlemen inquisitive, sir.'

'Brazilian gentlemen?' James found himself impatient as Lombardo seemed to swallow heavily and find the view of the town interesting. 'What Brazilian gentlemen? What are you talking about?'

'Why, the gentlemen from the sloop as sailed up just when we got back to the landing place.' Baines was all innocence now, but the hard light gleamed at the back of his eyes. 'Uniformed, they was. Got up like peelers in a comic opera. And they was there to see Senhor Henriques too, sir.'

'I must tell you, Senhor Onedin,' cut in Lombardo with a quick bright smile, 'that our next *musicale* to assist the opera house is to be graced with the presence of the famous Chiara Santa.'

'Fancy that, Lombardo,' responded James, for once prepared to indulge the little man's obsession. 'And who's Chiara Santa, eh?'

But Baines had more to say. The wind in the shrouds sang its song louder, as though anxious for the *Neptune* to cut short these pointless shorebound affairs and get back where she belonged, before a clean ocean blast. 'It seems the Emperor's made another decree about slavery. Brazil's a republic these days. But if the Emperor's to stay put, at least for the rest of his natural, then he's to use what's left of his authority to come down hard on slavers. And so he has done, sir. Slavers are to be pursued with the full force of the law . . . slavers, and them as profits from slavers' ways . . . '

'But why has she gone to South America, Uncle Robert? Why?' William frowned at the large, prosperous-looking figure opposite him. He remembered his mother's brother Robert as a big man, but he seemed now to have become quite huge. His office, in the great, rambling departmental store with its stucco façade and Greek pediment supported by a stone mermaid and merman, was opulent, and his clothes were of the best. He might have been what indeed he was these days, a merchant prince.

'Your mother did not confide in me in that particular.' Robert waved a fragrant cigar in the air. One always had to spare time for family, and it was pleasant no doubt to see this young son of Elizabeth's again. But the boy might remember he was a busy man. He had opened a new store in Birmingham only this week. And shortly before that, as everyone knew, the fine one in Manchester. 'I recall she was very worried about what had happened to your Uncle James. He's ruined now, you know. Ruined.' Robert shook his head soberly. There was reticence in his speech, for the word was no longer entirely proper in this office, these successful surroundings.

'You mean she's gone to help my Uncle James, Uncle Robert? But in what way?'

'Lord knows, lad. What brings you back to England, anyway? We thought you'd all settled in the far Antipodes. The Australian branch of the family.' Robert grinned at the boy across from him. It was necessary to get his mind off these gloomy thoughts. James was beyond help, poor devil. That was what came of overplaying your hand. Robert would never risk all in the manner his brother had done. His stores were going to be an empire one day. He had sold out his holdings in the Onedin Line Ltd. while he could still get a good price for them. That had been wise. Now that, in spite of all Tupman's care, news was beginning to get about that the South American venture had been a total disaster, shares were seriously depressed.

'I must go to Mother,' said William simply. 'It's what I came back to do. Brazil, you say?'

'She's left Port Baines, as it was called. Some queer place she's gone on to. Wait a bit. There was a letter said summat about it.' Robert opened a drawer in his ornate desk. He supposed if he told William all he could, then he would go away and leave him to his commercial preoccupations. A

121

chain of stores all over the country! London soon! And all this from a man who'd begun life as a humble ship's chandler!

The day outside the office windows was bright and clear. William stared out, and thought again of his father and Chiara Santa. There was a curious sense in which Daniel Fogarty was no real part of his life. He had not even come to know Daniel as his father until he was a young adult, and then he had simply responded to a rich man's generosity. He quite saw that now. His father had gone to remarkable lengths to prove to his son that he cared for him. He had in fact demonstrated that he cared for his son more than he cared for his son's mother. Elizabeth's face floated into William's mind: abused, neglected, betrayed.

'Manaos,' declared Robert with a grunt, looking at a letter. 'Place called Manaos.' Sometimes when he moved and bent sharply these days, as to the drawer in the ornate desk, it caused a little shortness of breath. He supposed it was the way he worked, never sparing himself. 'She says here it's a modern city, but near enough to a thousand miles up a river. That's a mighty exaggeration.' Robert could recognise feminine overstatement reliably enough. There could be no such thing as a city a thousand miles up a river. Was the Mersey of such length? And that, as everybody knew, was one of the world's major waterways.

'Manaos.' William frowned. 'Is that where Uncle James went too?'

'It seems so. Lord knows why.' Robert shrugged. It was getting near lunchtime, and he did not particularly want to invite William to share a meal with him. At his club, the Cadogan, they made a delicious steak, mushroom and oyster pie, and it was his habit to lunch on this with his chief accountant, who would murmur to him the while civilised tales of profit. 'But you can't go there too. Heathen place. Bound to be. Your mother'd want you to steer clear of it.'

'My mother's in this heathen place as you call it herself,'

replied William in the simple tone again,' and I must be with my mother. Manaos ... '

When dawn broke the morning after they had been stranded, Elizabeth, Letty and Charlotte found themselves in barren, flat land, wooded only in patches or with single scattered trees. They were almost on top of an extensive copse, from which the noises of the night must have proceeded. But in general there seemed to be only coarse, gritty sand, stretching featureless miles to the west of them. To eastward there was the river, broad and grey, the opposite bank out of sight. Of the *Lady Elizabeth*, which must have lain somewhere off here while they were brought ashore, there was no sign, and the expanse of water was empty of other craft of any sort.

'We can't stay here,' said Charlotte, looking anxiously about her. 'The cloud is breaking up. It will be abominably hot soon. There'll be no protection from the sun.'

'For pity's sake, where are we to go?' Letty's voice was sharp, and her eyes had a bright, distinctly unstable look. 'They've murdered us. As surely as if they'd taken up knives and stabbed us.'

'Please, Letty. Will you stop saying that?' Charlotte ran a quick hand through her hair. Despite her deliberate calm aboard ship, she could by no stretch of the imagination have been called at ease on this first morning as a castaway.

'Don't tell me what to say and what not to say!' Letty's voice was harsh and shrill now. 'As I recall it, your father wished me to correct *your* manners. I have done my best to comply with that injunction over a number of years now. I very much fear however – '

'Letty. Charlotte.' Elizabeth cut into the interchange in a deliberately controlled voice. 'That sort of thing is really quite pointless. We must save our energy for dealing with our situation. It is not entirely hopeless, I believe.' Her head had a defiant tilt as she surveyed their surroundings in the clear light of day. In the far distance, to landward, hills rose. They appeared to be barren ridges for the most part, blown bare by the winds off the plains, or strange, conical peaks, lifting sharply from the bleak surface. No point in trekking that way, then. 'If we were to gather wood, we might be able to start a fire.' Her mind had grasped at a notion, and it was a sound one. 'That would attract the attention of any passing ship.'

'How would we light a fire?' The shrill edge was still in Letty's tone. 'We've nothing to do that with. Isn't it better we think of what we're to eat? Those murderers put us ashore here so that we'd starve. Perhaps we shall starve. There may be nothing that can be eaten in this godforsaken place.'

'There are edible nuts,' replied Charlotte quietly. 'Everywhere along the Amazon there are edible nuts. We can make a little search in the wood there in a moment. In the meantime, Aunt Elizabeth, if you want to light a fire . . . I brought a tinder box with me.'

'Charlotte! Bless my soul, what made you think of that?' This time in Letty's voice there was something that Elizabeth could have taken for sarcasm. Was this ordeal, however it turned out, only to aggravate Letty's now undisguised distaste for her stepdaughter? Would mutual suffering only serve to drive them farther apart?

But Charlotte seemed aware of no overtone. Her anxiety proceeded not so much from dismay at their situation as from doubt of herself. 'I think my father would have remembered a tinder box in an impasse such as ours,' said Charlotte in a quiet voice once more. 'I set myself to thinking as he would from the moment I knew we were going to be tried.'

Tried. Elizabeth savoured the strangeness of the term as the three of them gathered wood for a beacon. James perhaps thought of life as a sort of test of abilities and resources too. But he had few of Charlotte's wider sympathies. He was in fact selfish and confined where she was outgoing and generous, which explained how he could have been so insensitive to the situation of his wife and daughter in Sao Paulo, while Charlotte had thought only of his difficulties.

'Look,' invited Charlotte, returning from the copse with firewood. She held out a small hollow of wood.

'What is it?' Elizabeth had already torn her dress in several places. She thought it absurd the clothes her society forced women to wear. The only effect of voluminous skirts and bodices was to unfit them for even the most elementary manual task. For almost the first time in her successful years, she felt a little pang of sympathy for skivvies.

'I think it's a bowl. Such as the forest Indians use.'

'Forest Indians in these parts? But there's nothing here.'

Half an hour later, they saw a sail far out on the water. It was only a small vessel, a trader's *cuberta*, but in quick excitement they ignited the beacon and began to shout. Their voices were little more than whispers in the huge emptiness however, and it was impossible to say whether the trader noticed the smoke from their fire or not. The wood was spongy and did not burn well.

'He must have seen it!' cried Letty, who had strained her throat yelling, as though there were some genuine hope of being heard. 'He must have!'

'Perhaps he did,' responded Charlotte. 'But he would have thought it was Indians.'

'Indians! Oh, you and your Indians!' Letty swung on her, frustrated and hurt to see rescue sliding away far across the water. 'I really don't understand your interest in these savages. Neither did your father. Your idiotic feeling for them in the past caused you to meet with an injury. Brought all our distresses upon us. It even caused your father and I – ' She broke off and averted her face. Elizabeth, also upset to observe the sail vanishing, knew she had almost said 'to find out the truth about ourselves' or 'to face facts.'

125

They got more wood and rebuilt the fire, but no other ships appeared that day. It was the sort of region vessels would probably get through as fast as possible, and preferably at night. Now that the sun had fully emerged, it was clear that it was a fearfully hot and exposed terrain. The name 'Dry Campos' was not without significance. They retired to the shelter of the wood and found some nuts to eat, just as Charlotte had predicted. But these were tiny and bitter, and Elizabeth, ravenous after her toil, realised they would have to find something more substantial the next day or be seriously weakened.

Night came down remarkably quickly, a velvet curtain drawn over their unfamiliar surroundings. The noises of the jungle began again. All three women asked themselves the question they dared not frame: whether there was anything else in the shadows as hungry as they were.

They woke early. It was extraordinary, Elizabeth thought, how when you are really tired, you can rest anywhere. The ground was in fact cushioned by a thick carpet of fallen leaves, years old by now. But it was hard compared to the bunks they had been banished from. Charlotte had roused and exerted herself earlier. It seemed she had found a spring deeper in the trees where at least they could drink and wash. She had also found more of the wooden hollows.

'There you are,' she announced, displaying one of her trophies proudly. 'Indians *have* been here.'

'Charlotte dear, why?' Elizabeth was secretly glad her niece had thought of the strong comb when they had been rudely separated from their ship. It made her feel inexplicably less hungry to be able to tidy her hair.

'I can't tell for sure. Perhaps because there are fish in this section of the river that they can't catch anywhere else. I saw fish skeletons. It's true. And I found this.' Charlotte held up a long straight shaft of bamboo, fashioned to a slender point at one end.

'A spear?' If Letty had felt well enough after a night of

only fitful sleep and gnawing apprehension she would have managed to sound contemptuous. 'Child, your Indians must be very strange savages if they catch fish with a spear.'

'The *Mura* Indians do just that,' answered Charlotte, as though they were in some kind of lesson and it were an important academic point. 'I read about it. They float bait on the water and wait in the shallows with their spears, and when the fish rise to it they spear them.' Charlotte pondered. 'If it's *Muras* who come to the neighbourhood, you know, we really ought to try and find them. They're nomads, so they'd know how to guide us to civilisation. They make a sort of snuff from certain seeds which apparently makes them drunk when they use it. That sounds very odd.'

Letty moaned gently. She ached in every limb after a night on the hard ground, and was clearly asking herself how long the anthropology lecture was to continue. Elizabeth also thought it misplaced. Charlotte turned to go. 'I'll be back in five minutes to show you the way to the spring. I'm looking for good, unbroken *lianas*. Those woody vines, you know?'

'Charlotte, what are you doing?' Elizabeth tossed her head. With her hair flowing free and untangled down her back, she was able to resume a touch of authority.

'Oh, the *lianas* are to bind the logs I've found together,' said Charlotte, stopping. 'The wood here floats better than it burns. So I'm making a raft. We'll be able to journey down river with the flow. Well, those *Muras* can't be far away,' she explained as the other two women looked blank. 'We've really very little hope of stopping a ship, it strikes me. So we must learn how to survive. Survive.'

She went on her way, and Letty merely shook her head wearily and painfully. But Elizabeth thought realistically that young Charlotte would indeed survive in this hostile terrain: and that if she and Letty wanted to do the same, they had better go along with her initiative.

As a consequence they helped with the making of the raft. From the outset it was clear that Charlotte knew what she

127

was doing, though where she had acquired such a skill remained a mystery. The thing sailed remarkably well as long as it was kept to the shallows and away from the powerful mainstream, where it would quickly have been whirled away and tossed over like a cork, drowning its passengers. The three castaways made remarkable progress through the Dry Campos region. It seemed depressingly alike everywhere, and if Indians did come to it they surely could never have stayed long.

They were lucky on the first day of their passage downstream to find a little belt of jungle in which there grew a Cow Tree. This was what Charlotte called it at once, though she also knew a longer native name for it. It was a huge tree with ragged red bark, and when this bark was stripped and squeezed, it produced milk. Elizabeth and Letty were astonished. The liquid looked exactly like milk and tasted similar too, though sweeter and richer. Letty felt ill for taking somewhat more than the others, and when some of the liquid was put aside in one of the bowls it rapidly developed the consistency of glue. But it was nourishing. In addition some genuine 'Brazil' nuts were found, enclosed in the enveloping cups in which they grew. The party felt distinctly better, and journeyed on with sustenance of this sort for three days.

On the fourth day, they entered into a coastal region which seemed to consist of primeval forest. The straggling flat plains of the Dry Campos were no more, and giant trees rose out of fertile dark soil, stretching away in green and dense profusion to the far distant hills. When the women dragged their raft ashore for the night, they found that within a very few feet they were hemmed in by jungle.

'We'd better not go too far from the river,' adjudged Charlotte, looking carefully above and around her. 'I've read that in this sort of country, you only have to go a tiny distance to be utterly lost. You lose bearings.'

'Dear Charlotte,' responded Letty, who was better in her-

self now. 'What in the world should we do without you?'
Elizabeth heard no ambiguous resonances this time. It is
curious how when existence is reduced to the simplest and
most spartan elements, it often brings out the best in those
who might most be supposed to resent and resist its hard
demands on them.

Then, almost at once, Letty gave a scream. She clapped
a terrified hand to her mouth, and stared ahead. Elizabeth
and Charlotte quickly followed her gaze.

A group of people had appeared at the bole of a tree that
could have been twenty-five feet in circumference. They
seemed to have come from behind the monster, from somewhere deeper in the forest. They were short and at first
glance unfavoured. The bodies of the men were begrimed
with black mud. The women wore a scrap of cloth about the
loins but otherwise were naked, as were the children. There
were perhaps a dozen of them in all and they were absolutely
still, making no sound.

CHAPTER NINE

Charlotte was the first to break the silence. She took a pace or two towards the Indians, scarcely assured in attitude, and addressed them hesitantly in a tongue of which neither of the other women understood a word. The Indians gave no sign of comprehending, though Elizabeth thought she saw a brief look of what could have been perplexity or surprise flicker across the face of the man who seemed to be leading the group. But it was a momentary thing, so fleeting as perhaps not to have been there at all. The Indians seemed able to withhold all facial expression. Their eyes were no more than points of light in impassive masks, and they were so still that they might have been statues.

When Charlotte had finished, nobody stirred. The girl waited a moment, then backed away from them. Elizabeth saw the beginnings of tears in her eyes. She moved quickly to her niece and put a supportive arm around her. It had been a brave attempt. 'Oh, Aunt Elizabeth,' whispered Charlotte in distress. 'They don't understand me.'

'There, there, child. Perhaps they won't harm us.'

'They shouldn't be violent,' Charlotte informed her with a frown. 'Not if they're *Mura* Indians. Nomads, you see. A family of them. And that mud the men put on their bodies . . . ' All at once this extraordinary girl seemed confident again. She quickly wiped away her tears. 'It's to keep the mosquitoes from stinging them when they go hunting near the river. Yes, of course . . . they're *Muras* . . . '

The man who seemed to be leader of the group stepped forward. Letty, who still had her hand to her mouth, stifled a further cry of fright. But the man stopped again, peered at Charlotte in what seemed a severe manner, and then addressed her very rapidly in the same unintelligible tongue. Elizabeth could not tell if her niece understood what was being said or not. After a little however, her face lit up and she smiled. It was a smile in which relief, amazement and delight were mingled in equal proportions.

'Oh, Aunt Elizabeth! Letty!' cried Charlotte happily. 'He's asking us if we live here. He wants to know if we're hungry!'

What followed was confusing but deeply reassuring. On Charlotte's conveying to the man that no, she and her companions did not live there, and yes, they were dreadfully hungry, the man rapped something at the women with the children, who without further bidding began to build a fire. The children went and got flat stones of more or less the same size from the river's edge, erecting them into a kind of cairn against the fire, which thus became a rudimentary oven.

The men meantime went down to the water's edge and began to point in various directions, chattering volubly. The river here gave out into a series of ponds, some deep, some no larger than puddles. They seemed to be trying to select one of the larger ones. At length a pond was chosen, and one of the men dived into it, disappearing beneath the surface for what seemed a considerable time. Suddenly he broke water again, baring white teeth in a great laugh and shouting to his companions. Two other men dived into the water as well, and the swimmer took a huge gulp of air, disappearing beneath the surface again.

When next they emerged they were all three together, and clung on to a large, threshing creature which turned out to

131

be a turtle. They had caught it by the simple expedient of diving down and grabbing its back legs. The unfortunate beast writhed and struggled, but had no chance against the experienced fishers. The Indians dragged their prize ashore and seized heavy sticks, beginning to beat it to death. Charlotte looked quickly away.

But the turtle meat, once it had been roasted in the primitive oven, was the most delicious food the Englishwomen had ever tasted. Elizabeth thought it strange and contrary that in this uncivilised place their very lives should have been saved by something that at home would probably have been regarded as a luxury, made into a gourmet meal and served with great ceremony and expense. It was pleasantly warm where they sat and ate, shaded from the fierce sun by the massive trees, and after their meal she felt drowsy. Elizabeth had almost dropped off when she became aware of Letty speaking.

'Can we trust them?' she was asking. The food appeared to have given her a new alertness, and she was regarding the Indians near the fire with wary suspicion. 'I don't understand them. They don't seem in the least surprised to have come across us here.'

'They're quite used to Europeans, Letty,' responded Charlotte. She too seemed drowsy. 'All up and down the Amazon the native people know about the white man. The question really is, can they trust us?'

'When I want to be contradicted I'll tell you as much, child,' snapped Letty, the governess again. She was unquestionably revived by a decent meal. 'Can you give me a reason, since you claim to know so much about them, why they're being so pleasant to us unless it means they intend to have the price of it later?'

'The simple fact could be we represent no threat to them,' said Charlotte simply. She was nervous of Letty's sarcasm and querulousness. She had been exposed to them once before, and remembered the distress of mind too well. 'We're not armed like the traders are. We're defenceless. And we're women.'

Charlotte rose from where she sat and ran her hands briskly through her hair. She had decided she did not want to sleep just now. She smoothed down her dress – a pointless action since like Elizabeth's it was torn and grimy – and moved to the headman of the Indian group again. There were matters to be conveyed, arrangements to be made.

'Women,' echoed Letty as Charlotte once more addressed the headman hesitantly in his own language. 'Yes, she speaks the truth there, no doubt. Nobody fears women. Women don't command much respect in the world, savage or civilised.' And she nodded briefly to the Indian women with the children. They sat apart from their menfolk, subservient and silent. They had not eaten themselves until the men had had their choice of the cooked turtle meat.

'Letty,' said Elizabeth. She still felt very sleepy, and it was an effort to keep awake. 'Why do you hate Charlotte so?'

'I don't hate Charlotte. Please try not to be ridiculous, Elizabeth.'

'You suppose James prefers her to you,' went on the other woman. 'And that makes you over-critical of her. But is it true?' The drowsy Elizabeth had no idea why she was talking like this and in such a place. She could only suppose that the banishing of the dread fear of starvation from her mind had freed it for whatever else might be concerning her.

'Of course it's true!' Letty experienced no reluctance in talking of the matter. If anything she seemed anxious to unburden herself. 'James said so. On the night of the hurricane, that terrible night in Port Baines, he shouted at me because I hadn't prevented Charlotte from going to her precious Indians. He *blamed* me for it. As if there were anything I could have done!' Letty remained indignant, but there was a kind of sadness in her too. 'Such a wilful, self-opinionated child . . . James took her side against me as often as not, you know. He wasn't consistent. He disliked his daughter going near the Indians. Disliked it a great deal. But he didn't tell her that. He simply waited until it could be represented as my fault. I was expendable. Because I wasn't Anne...'

It was private where they sat. The irregular sounds of talk just across from them did not disturb. Benevolent light filtered down through the trees. Elizabeth's weary eyes seemed to behold Letty's angular face as something softer than it usually appeared. There was a vulnerable human being behind the stern façade, as capable as any other of hurt and dismay. Elizabeth wondered if there was not in fact a strong beauty in the face.

'Anne,' murmured Letty softly. A wry smile turned the corners of her mouth. 'It's Anne I should hate if I hate any-body. Poor, dead Anne. Because she lives on in James' heart. If I'm hard to Charlotte it's Anne's fault. No one else's. Charlotte is what he had from Anne. Anne, who stands between me and my husband...'

The fogs of sleep were slowly but inevitably engulfing Elizabeth. Her eyelids dropped. 'Why did he marry me, do you suppose?' The voice came to her as from a great dis-tance. 'What was the sense in that? If he only wanted some-body to look after Charlotte, he could just have kept me on as a governess. I had no other plans. But when he proposed marriage to me... I thought that was because he wanted me for myself...'

The last conscious thought Elizabeth had was that that was precisely what she had thought when she had married Daniel Fogarty. Daniel Fogarty, from whom she had had William...

'You want to join your mother?' queried James in a mysti-fied voice. 'You journeyed from Australia to England to do so? And then when you found she wasn't in Liverpool, you came all the way to South America? Manaos – ?'

'It's where she was supposed to be,' answered William reasonably. 'The letter to Uncle Robert said so. Manaos.'

'Aye.' They walked one of the new thoroughfares of the city. The duckboards were still down since the paving stones were laid only in sections here, and it was the rainy season. On the previous evening a positive deluge had broken over Manaos. The *igarapes* were monstrously swollen, and elegantly attired men and women picked their way over a sea of mud like wading birds. 'But she's not arrived so far, William. Lord knows why. Maybe she's changed her mind.'

The confused James could not hazard a guess as to why this young nephew of his should suddenly turn up in the depths of the Amazonian jungle. It had been bad enough that Elizabeth was not where she had a right to be, in distant Australia. What had happened in that *ultima thule*, that its denizens had rudely taken to appearing on the other side of the world? When people went to the colonies it was generally all one heard of them until the sad notification, years later, of their passing.

'I don't understand why Mother wanted to come to this place,' confessed William, looking dubiously about him. The houses and buildings that were finished seemed extravagant and out of place. Even more so than in fashionable Sydney, vulgarity and pretension ruled. This was a city of the *nouveau riche*. 'Uncle Robert said it was something to do with you.'

'Nothing to do with me.' James' tone was firm, for he was quite clear in his mind that that was the way it was going to be. 'I see to myself. I don't need help, or even attention paid. Remember it, lad. Here's the place I told you of.'

James stopped and indicated ahead of him. An absurdly ornate arch entwined with plaster leaves offered entry to a heavy white edifice that might have been transported from a European resort such as Biarritz or Nice. 'You can stay

135

here. It's a hotel as fine as any you'd encounter in Liverpool. Better, some say.'

James got back to his dock office in an evil mood. He did not know precisely what he should do about young William. He had taken the boy to a hotel because he seemed to have money, and it relieved him of the embarrassment of having to entertain him. James lived very simply in Manaos, unlike his peers. When he needed to make a display for business purposes, he took rooms at the same hotel to which he had despatched William, and stinted nothing. Otherwise he sacrificed himself to the everyday privations of amassing wealth. Now that the truly astonishing profits of rubber were beginning to come in, he began to see the wood despite the trees. Given luck, he even believed that within measurable time he would restore his fortune *in toto*.

'G'day to you, sir.' Baines snapped a salute as James entered the office. Lombardo was off somewhere on business, and Baines was in a corner occupied with what looked like bills of lading. There was still a gruffness, a distance in him. The matter of Henriques and his methods lay like a ravine between the two men. James avoided consideration of the matter, believing that sooner or later it would be resolved by default. Baines shared no such confidence.

'I think we'd best take Master William with us when we go downstream,' stated James, moving to his desk.

'Why would that be, sir?' Baines looked up from his papers, surprised. He was still in Manaos because after he had brought the *Neptune* there against orders, she had been found in need of repairs. James had in any case already arranged for another ship to stand by at Para, and was organising a regular shuttle to deal with the quantities of rubber he was now handling. But the *Neptune* was now seaworthy again and ready to go back into service.

'Because I've a duty to keep some sort of eye on William. Blood's thicker than water. And it should interest him, seeing how the rubber trade is conducted.'

'There's things in that trade as'd rouse the interest of a deep sleeper,' rejoined Baines dourly. 'Yet we'll not take Master William to the landing place served by Senhor Henriques, sir. I'll not be calling at the landing place any road.'

James blinked up at the mariner from his desk. The dock office was small and crowded, and the constant racket of the donkey engine of the flying fox without was often enough to obscure what people were saying. James presumed he had misheard.

But Baines shot a hard glance at his employer. His eye was fiery and determined. 'I'm lawful master of the *Neptune*,' he prefaced his remarks as before, 'and I'm telling you now, Captain Onedin, any time as my ship is to be put at the disposal of slavers and their traffic –'

'My God, Baines –'

'I don't care if Henriques returns from wherever he's vanished to with all the rubber in Brazil,' Baines ran on loudly. 'You may care to run the gauntlet of the law personal, but you've no right to expect me to do likewise. Yet it ain't only a question of the law. I must say I'm surprised at you, sir.' Baines adopted a harsher tone. 'Surprised and ashamed. You, who fought so hard in your day for the Plimsoll line on ships, so that honest sailormen'd not be condemned to certain drowning when coffin ships foundered. You, who paid fair wages to crew on your vessels, no matter how it grieved you to part with what was necessary. And now you'd not only take what a filthy slaver acquired for you, but complain when he's not there with a bigger and richer consignment, all wrung out of the hides of poor ignorant savages.'

An angry reply sprang to James' lips, but he quickly suppressed it. This needed careful handling. James had no idea if Henriques had disappeared forever, or if he was simply waiting till the coast was clear after the surprise visit of the police. But if Henriques did return, James knew he wanted the rubber he could supply. He could hardly expect Baines

137

to sympathise with the point of view. Baines after all was not a businessman. Baines was not an *entrepreneur*.

'Wages,' murmured James, deliberately keeping his tone steady. 'You'd have me pay wages direct to the Indians. As though they were seafarers. But it's naught like that. Half of them think work itself has been abolished – do you recall Lombardo telling us that? So I must leave people like Henriques to make their own arrangements in their own world. Otherwise there'd be money paid out and no work done. And where would my profit be then?'

'Your profit! God above, sir, do you never think of a mortal thing outside your profit?' Baines was barking now, hugely angry.

Anger in the giant faintly scared James. But he could check his true feeling no more. 'You've done well enough by it in your time,' he struck back.

'Not any longer. No, sir, not one moment longer.' Baines dropped to the floor a paper he still held and advanced on the desk, bringing his ham of a fist down on it. 'I don't give you your argument, that ignorant savages think work has been abolished, and so slaving's nobody's business but his who's holding slaves. That way it'd be right to say murder's nobody's business but his who's doing murder. I'll load no more tainted goods for you, Captain Onedin. You may fill your holds with purest gems if you wish, but while they're suspect I'll carry them nowhere.'

'You're mad.' James was bewildered. 'You're master of the *Neptune*. You'll ply where and carry whatever I say.'

'I resign her, sir. Haven't you grasped my meaning? I give you back your damned command.' James' bewilderment turned to incredulity. For Baines this surely indicated a final state of mind. The *Neptune* was his life. He loved her as other men love women and others (like James Onedin) love riches. 'I'll finish this trip back to England and sign off with the humblest crewman. I'm beaching myself on a lee shore.'

Baines swung away for the door. James for the moment could lay his tongue to no word, no comment. The giant saw the paper that had dropped to the floor and swept it up. 'My duty to give this to you, sir,' he announced with forced calm. 'Message to say a steam packet named the *Lady Elizabeth*, bearing her owner, one Lady Elizabeth Fogarty, docked at Para above three weeks ago.'

'Three weeks?' James blinked. He took the proffered paper and stared at it. 'Then why isn't Elizabeth in Manaos yet?'

'That's the question, sir. The *Lady Elizabeth* left port on the date shown there, under a master called Furtado.'

It made even less sense to James. Then it came to him. 'Why, she can't have sailed for Manaos, obviously.' In spite of his upset at Baines' attitude, James found himself oddly relieved. He had not been looking forward to Elizabeth's arrival. Or was it Letty's coming he dreaded? He would not answer his own question. 'She must have turned a hundred and eighty degrees, gone back on her tracks. Aye. Changed her mind.'

'Authorities think this Furtado or whoever he is could be someone they're interested in, sir.'

'Why?'

'Don't say. Just there in the message.'

'Elizabeth's a shrewd woman,' ruminated James. 'Well able to look after herself. Look. If her steam packet's in the river complex, it must have called in somewhere after Para. In which case we'd have a report of that docking too. But there's no such report. Therefore she must be back at sea – '

There was the click of the dock office door closing. James frowned. Baines had again vanished, believing his duty done. James could still not quite believe what the most dedicated sailor he had ever known had told him a moment before. Baines giving up his command, leaving the sea, just because a few Indians had been forced into serving a grasping white master – ? It seemed out of all conscience.

James had a sudden vision of himself standing by while a tall man on a donkey cart loaded with rubber cracked a long whip over a huddle of frightened Indians. His daughter Charlotte was there, weeping, and Letty too, her face a mask. Letty asked nothing of him in this matter. She was clearly waiting on some more important issue.

Elizabeth, Charlotte and Letty journeyed through the jungle for more than a week with the *Muras* who had befriended them. They had little choice in this, for though they had at first insisted on travelling close to the river, they had attracted the attention of no craft that they saw, no matter how they screeched or lighted fires. And alone, they could scarcely have hoped to forage adequately.

Charlotte had conveyed to the headman the desire of all three of them to get back among their own people. But though this was understood, neither the headman nor other members of the group appeared anxious to approach European settlements. They seemed to walk in fear of the white man.

The country they traversed was all primitive forest now. The Indians at night constructed make-shift shelters of fallen branches and fronds, but Elizabeth discovered it was possible to be safe and warm in the 'chambers' at the base of the greatest trees. These were formed by the roots, which had emerged ridge-like from the earth as the tree got ever higher, thus creating roomy spaces underneath. They were capacious enough to accommodate five or six people, and Elizabeth felt safer in such a retreat from the nocturnal animals that they were accustomed to hear all through the hours of darkness.

Animal life even by day was a hazard. The flocks of toucans, perched high up in the trees, unnerved them with their unexpected, yelping cries. Stinging flies descended on them in clouds, and they trod on lizards if they were not

140

careful. There were heavy brown spiders, hanging somnolent in webs between trees, ready to move and strike at a touch. But worst of all were the ants.

The first time they encountered these, Letty was a little ahead of the other two women on a forest 'path' known to the Indians. All at once the headman, who had been out of sight, came pounding back bellowing something in his own tongue. The other Indians in the little column scattered with cries of alarm, vanishing as though simply absorbed into the trees around. Letty could not understand what was happening. 'Charlotte!' she cried back to her stepdaughter. 'What is it?'

'I don't know, Letty . . .'

The ground immediately ahead of them began gently to heave as if it were the sea. Inexplicably, the undergrowth lifted like a wave, rippling and thrusting towards them. Higher growth, young trees, were toppled out of the way, falling aside. Only the mighty jungle giants seemed able to resist the extraordinary drive and swell of the land.

And then they saw clearly. A great procession of tiny creatures was approaching them, millions of individuals, spread in a phalanx perhaps fifty yards wide. They moved powerfully and relentlessly, carrying all before them. It still took a second to recognise them as ants, for they were much bigger than the European variety, some of them perhaps three inches in length. The headman appeared again among the trees far to the right of the three women, howling and beckoning at them to hurry.

'Quickly,' shouted Charlotte. 'Quickly!'

Letty, Elizabeth and Charlotte raced for the headman. Letty caught her foot in a tangle of creeper and fell heavily. She screamed in terror. Elizabeth, nearest her, quickly dragged her to her feet and hauled her on. Their clothing, already in shreds, was torn even further. Distraught, frightened out of their wits, with Letty in hysterics, they finally got clear of the column of ants. It went straight ahead on its path, deviating not an inch. Had they stayed where they were, they would have been picked bones by now.

As Letty still sobbed, Elizabeth looked at her rags of clothes and shuddered. Really, so much in this world was beyond endurance. Of her dress, there was hardly enough left for decency.

The whole question of decency arose a day or two later in a fuller way. The Indian women wore only their loincloths, and those not at all times. Alone among their own sex they went completely naked. Elizabeth, cursing as she had done from the beginning the stupid garments her society forced her to wear, envied them. When their wanderings brought them to a forest pond, the Indian women would strip off whatever rags they had on at the time and leap into the water, laughing and sporting with their children.

It was the afternoon they came to the waterfall that Elizabeth decided British standards of decency had been observed long enough. It was a beautiful spot, which the Indians seemed to have visited before. The water fell a clear thirty feet from the stream above, forming a deep crystal pool. Elizabeth waited till the Indian women had finished washing and gone off to join their men, who were busy making the strange snuff that their tribe from time to time manufactured. It seemed to be some kind of festival day. The snuff was produced from seeds of a particular plant, which were laboriously ground until the result was a fine powder.

With the Indians occupied, Elizabeth gently slid off what remained of her dress and entered the water. Charlotte had agreed to accompany her, but Letty was having none of it. 'No,' she declined firmly. 'We will sooner or later come to European habitation. That will be the time to wash. In fitting privacy.'

Once in the water, Elizabeth and Charlotte first cleansed their grimy and ragged clothes. Then they spread them on the banks of the pool to dry and went back into the cool,

142

kindly element, happily and sensuously detached from the world.

They had been there hardly more than five minutes when Letty all at once gave a sharp cry, pointing. Two of the Indian men had unexpectedly arrived on the other side of the pool. They were staring at the Englishwomen in the water and making gestures. Elizabeth realised with a little gasp that in the clear pool their bodies must have been perfectly visible to the intruders. The men seemed to be behaving strangely into the bargain. They were laughing and swaying, almost as though they were drunk. It must have been true then, that their snuff had alcoholic properties.

'Go away!' shouted Letty, as though shooing troublesome dogs from a kitchen. 'Go away, I say!'

But the men continued to laugh and sway. They were shouting things over their shoulders now. Elizabeth did not think they were consumed so much by the stirrings of lust as by simple amusement. It came to her that the sight of pale, pink bodies in the water must have seemed to them distinctly risible: they might even have thought that European women were brown underneath their voluminous garments, merely painting the exposed parts of their bodies. Attracted by the noise, other Indians appeared at the pool side, and also started to laugh. Elizabeth began to be annoyed. It was one thing to be slavered over, perhaps, quite another to be treated as an object of derision.

With a final howl of laughter, the two original watchers hurled themselves into the water. Letty duly screamed, and Elizabeth and Charlotte at once struck for the bank and their dresses. It was going too far. They got safely away from their snuff-inebriated observers, but as they scampered into the protecting jungle, grabbing at their rags, there was the loudest laughter of all. Elizabeth glumly appreciated that it must have been their pink bottoms which produced it, wobbling incongruously away from the onlookers into the mercifully enveloping green.

Late one day the women and Indians came to a clearing near the river bank. Elizabeth was tired and Letty utterly exhausted. It had been a particularly hard trek, over country that rose and fell steeply. But Charlotte seemed to think they should set about building a beacon without delay. They had seen that day two ships out on the great flow, and the headman had conveyed to her that he had now come as close as he was likely to to anything approaching a European settlement. They had to attract attention.

It was while the weary women were collecting firewood that a great shouting began among the Indians. One man who had been foraging in the jungle ran back into the clearing, yelling something indistinguishable. Others at once emerged from the trees too, and there was the unexpected sound of rifle shots.

A tubby European in a straw hat rushed into the clearing. He held a rifle. Then a negro in European clothes appeared from the opposite side, also armed. He fired a resounding shot into the air, to prevent the Indians bolting again. The Indian women and children screamed, huddling together. The men looked desperately for avenues of escape. There seemed to be none.

The enveloping bush fell apart, and a stringy man on a tall black horse thudded into the clearing. The horse whinnied and reared as it was reined in, and the rider surveyed the Indians with a bright but bleak eye. Then his gaze fell on Elizabeth and the two other white women, and he gaped unbelievingly. He quickly dismounted and hastened across to them. He seemed a well-enough attired man. But all he could manage was something rapid in Portuguese. Charlotte recognised it as a baffled 'What does this mean – what does this mean?'

Elizabeth felt acutely conscious of her rags. The man's penetrating eyes were on her. 'Thank goodness,' she muttered. 'Thank goodness. We were – shipwrecked. We have had a terrible time. We have had to depend on the Indians for everything.'

'Then that is at an end, senhora.' The man spoke English now. He whipped off his hat and made a deep bow to the three of them. 'Permit me to offer you my services. My name is Henriques.'

CHAPTER TEN

When James and Baines left Manaos with young William in the *Neptune*, the matter of Baines' relinquishing his command at the end of the voyage and the whole question of the landing place near Obydos was still an issue. Baines remained adamant. James could go ashore at the landing place if he chose, but Baines would not dock. He would simply lay to and turn his back if in fact James made it his business to search out any of the missing rubber and ferry it out by *cuberta*. He could not deny that much minimal co-operation to James as owner. But he would surely himself 'be no part'.

William on his side had been reluctant to come on the voyage downriver. His familiar hatred of the sea returned the moment he clapped eyes on the high masts and cross-trees of the *Neptune*. It was sailing vessels in particular that seemed to bring out the antipathy in him: a simple creak of timbers and lines, and he was again a sniffling boy in mid-shipman's uniform aboard one of England's last surviving wooden walls off Rock Ferry, hating it all and dreaming of his father. A father whom he had found, and had now in turn abandoned.

William had decided to go with James and Baines for the

146

very good reason that he had become considerably worried about his mother. James had told him of her ship docking at Para so long a time previously, but had dismissed William's fears for her safety by explaining that the Amazon traffic was different from that of the open sea. 'If anything ill befell her in river waters, lad,' James had informed him dourly, 'we'd've heard. There aren't so many big ships ply up and down even such a mighty waterway as this, and one craft looks out for another constantly. No, she turned on her tail at Para, you mark my word. Went back home, like as not. Aye. She's taken Letty and Charlotte to Liverpool, that's what it is, and I'll have word of it any day now. Best thing for them now that Charlotte's well again. It would have been mad bringing them to Manaos. Mad.'

William was not so sure that his uncle was right about his mother. She had been hurt by his father, he saw now. Chiara Santa had represented a problem that had somehow diminished her, and she had had to get away from Australia to reassert her selfhood. She was unusual among women, her son realised, in that she had long been beholden to no husband, and could not now be put in a subservient position by one. In such a state of mind, she might well have taken foolish chances or embraced needless risks.

A day or so up the river, the *Neptune* passed the regular steamer between Para and Manaos. It was gusty and the vessels were considerably apart, barely in sight of each other. William could thus have had no way of guessing that aboard the steamer was Chiara Santa, journeying to Manaos to fulfil her singing engagement. He could also hardly have guessed that she was not alone, but had a travelling companion: his father, Sir Daniel Fogarty.

'Daniel, caro,' pleaded Chiara Santa, a brisk wind tossing her long black hair. 'Let us go below. It is evil weather.'

'Just trying to make out that brig over there,' answered

Daniel, indicating the square rigger on the horizon. 'The line of her seems familiar, somehow or other . . . '

'*Ebbene,*' Chiara assented. 'But my skin in this wind will become hard like leather and red and not pleasant. We shall be in Manaos tomorrow. I must begin to compose myself.'

Daniel grinned broadly at her. She found it impossible not to respond to his smiles now. They seemed to disarm her and render her helpless. Without warning, she felt watery at the knees. Really, she had better begin to compose herself at once.

Since Para, Chiara Santa had been in what she could only describe as a state of high excitement. After all, she had in no way expected to see Daniel Fogarty when she arrived at the river port. It had been a considerable shock. The voyage across the Pacific by steamer had been long and slow. Then she had had to endure a rough overland journey through a section of Colombia, and finally another steamer trip to the mouth of the Amazon. Yet when she had disembarked at Para, exhausted, there on the dock had been Daniel Fogarty, who had bidden her *bon voyage* when she left Sydney.

It was not in fact quite as miraculous as it seemed, though Chiara's Italian peasant forebears would undoubtedly have lighted candles and donated heavily to a jewelled crown for the madonna in the parish church at the thought of it. Daniel, aware that he was in Chiara's mind – she had in fact thought of little else but him over the tedious miles of ocean – and not wishing to be parted from her for so long, had chartered a fast schooner to take him over the same route as she was traversing. Spurred all the way by favourable winds, the schooner had unintentionally proved the superiority of sail over steam when the conditions were right. It was formidable. What did the world want? Steady, stodgy routine on the high seas, or the spirited and mercurial unpredictability of a smiling lover?

A lover. *E vero,* Chiara reflected somberly. There was

still the question of accepting love or remaining circumspect about it, of course. It seemed to put obligations on one, this action worthy of Don Giovanni at his most persistent. She wondered what the goddess would want of her now. But the goddess chose to be silent. Did that leave her free?

'I'd swear that ship was British,' murmured Daniel, gazing after the vanishing outline of the square rigger. 'British, and known to me . . .'

'Daniel, caro.' Chiara looked down at the grey water, rushing past them below. 'Why have you done this thing?'

'Done what?'

'Come to South America. Come after me.'

Daniel's reply was oddly cautious. 'I didn't think we'd finished our business,' he said.

He made it sound like some sort of commercial negotiation, she thought. Yet perhaps it was only to cover doubts that afflicted him even as they afflicted her. 'Have you ever wondered why I have never asked you about your wife?' she enquired.

'Chiara.' He had been leaning against the rail, but now straightened up, indicating the wide waste of water before them with a sweep of his hand. He made an imposing figure against the great river. 'Look out there. Do you know what it is? What it *represents*?'

'No.'

'Life between,' said Daniel. She plainly did not understand, so he continued. 'All journeys can be looked on as life between. There's what was, what mattered, when you began. There's what will be, what will matter, in the end. But in between . . . ' He shrugged. An especially sharp gust of wind took her hair again, flicking strands of it into her eyes. It barely stirred his crisp, curled locks. 'We can be sure of nothing, Chiara. You ask about my wife. Here. But here, she may not even exist.' Elizabeth's face came unbidden into his mind. He recalled how once he had loved her, yearned for her when she had been married to Albert

149

Frazer. It was a madness that was on him, then. An insane certainty. 'Here, she is . . . not relevant. Any more than your singing is. Your singing, my marriage – that is yesterday. That is tomorrow.'

She knew what he was saying, yet wished the goddess would respond in some way. Chiara had been allotted one of the best cabins aboard the river steamer, but it was a poky and confined place for all that. It occurred to her reflectively that if she were to leave the door unlocked of a night, even a little ajar, that would perhaps assist the goddess in the fashioning of her judgement. One dared not think for oneself. There was too much peril. Daniel Fogarty was a beautiful man. *Si, certe.* But when you are wedded to your art, and your art alone, perhaps you are required to settle for something more modest. Less distracting, anyway. Why, oh why, would the goddess not speak . . . ?

The reception in Manaos was rapturous. The whole town seemed to have turned out for Chiara Santa. She herself was astonished, and Daniel sobered. It was the return of the status quo – what was, what mattered – and an end of theorising. The Europeans wore their finery, and the *caboclos* or city Indians were arrayed as for a festival. This meant that the women had taken clothes off rather than donned them, going naked from the waist up. The men wore high feather crowns. Many of the young people of all races sang songs, accompanying themselves on the *cavaquinho*, a kind of viola in use everywhere.

Staring at the myriad canoes on the river, the press of people in their gay clothes under the bright sun, Chiara Santa found it hard to believe she was so well known. A disappointment lay in store for her in this respect. The citizens of Manaos, fixated upon their great opera house, certain that its construction would enhance their lives out of all imagination, had no choice but to worship a representative of the dream world. By far the majority had probably indeed never heard of Chiara Santa, any more than they had heard of Lilly Lehmann or even of Giuseppe Verdi. But it was necessary to greet such persons with fitting and extravagant honours.

With Chiara whisked off to her hotel and a grand banquet of greeting, waited on by men of substance in formal attire, Daniel found himself at a loose end. He had not wanted to be part of all the adulation and extravagance, an aspect of Chiara's theatrical life that he had never really been able to stomach. He went into a respectable enough looking tavern in the dock area and ordered two fingers of brandy.

'It is a local brandy, senhor,' confided a depressed-looking little man a distance from him, who had dressed up for the festivities but clearly found them wanting in some way. 'You must be careful.'

Daniel thanked him and enquired why he seemed so gloomy. 'Senhor,' replied the little man with an indifferent shrug, 'I have been promised a place at the grand banquet to greet the beauteous and talented Chiara Santa. I had already made certain concessions in the way of business for it. But at the last moment, senhor, I am told there is unfortunately no place for me after all. I offer twice the concessions, three times if necessary. But to no avail. Rich men control Manaos. Men richer by far than Lombardo.'

Daniel fell into easy conversation with the stranger, but it was some time before he discovered his connection with James Onedin. Then he simply could not believe it.

'James Onedin?' he echoed. 'You are in partnership in this place with James Onedin? My brother-in-law? But – but why? I don't understand. What on earth is he doing here?'

'He trades in rubber.'

'Rubber? What kind of a trade is rubber for a shipping man?'

'It is the most lucrative trade in the world. And Captain Onedin requires much money.'

Again it took Daniel a time to arrive at the fact that Port

Baines had been a dismal failure, that James had been nearly bankrupted and was now engaged in getting back on his feet before his creditors could foreclose on him.

'Well,' murmured Daniel thoughtfully, leaning back in his chair. Little Lombardo had been quite right, the local brandy was appalling. 'We heard little of the Port Baines venture in Australia. Only that there had been – reverses. Yes, there was some unspecified talk of that. But from what you say . . . ' Daniel had at the beginning invested heavily in Port Baines, principally with the idea of seizing control if he could. He had wanted to finally even the score with James Onedin. But James had defeated him in that simple ambition. Now it seemed to Daniel he could force James into ruin, something he had once dearly yearned for. Yet did it matter any more? Elizabeth in Liverpool would plainly be *au fait* with her brother's situation. Probably she had already extended to him as much financial protection as she could manage.

'*Perdao*, senhor.' Lombardo was speaking again. 'You say your name is – ah – Fogarty?'

'Yes. Why . . . ?'

'It is very strange.' Lombardo shook his head and gazed soulfully into the wine he was drinking. Would the divine Chiara Santa sing at the banquet? *Dis-moi que je suis belle* . . . He supposed not. 'You are perhaps connected with shipping?'

'I used to be. What's the matter?'

'We have had much news lately of a steamship called the *Lady Elizabeth*,' went on Lombardo soberly. 'She was pirated on the Amazon, pirated by a rascally fellow called Furtado, who has been a slaver and a murderer. He has now been caught and hanged in Pernambuco. But of the owner of this ship, who was aboard at the time of the pirating, there is no news. The owner was a woman, whose name is given as Lady Elizabeth Fogarty. Is this perhaps a kinswoman of yours, senhor?'

As the *Neptune* dropped anchor in the coastal waters south of Obydos, young William muttered a heartfelt prayer of thanks. He could not remember such an evil passage in all his brief years of hating the sea. A wind had arisen just east of the port of Serpa, and had increased in violence and bluster the more they had tried to run before it. Tacking to avoid being piled up on an invisible shore or dumped on one of the sandbanks that could occur without warning in these waters, Baines had shouted orders with zest from his poop and the hands had scrambled about high in the shuddering yards as though revelling in it. Even Uncle James, appearing at the hatch streaked with rain and windblown, had not looked put out by the adverse conditions.

William could not understand. He felt desperately ill, and even after the storm had blown itself out, did not quickly recover. When the *Neptune* was swinging at anchor and James came to him to say he was going ashore to search again for his agent in these parts, whose name seemed to be Henriques, William was green.

'Best get to your bunk with a toddy, lad,' muttered James, not used to this sort of thing on shipboard and tempted to believe it was sham anyway.

'No,' cried William in protest. It had been arranged that he should go ashore with James, and he was desperate to get off the *Neptune*, if only for a little while. He was certain it was the ship itself, an evil presence, a malevolent place, that was causing his ill health. 'I'm interested in how the rubber trade works, and I want to see.'

'May be nothing to see this trip. But as you prefer.' James understood the unhappy lubber needed the feel of solid earth under his feet again. He deplored such a characteristic, especially in a relative. But there you are, there were even those who said Horatio Nelson himself had begun life as a weakly, perpetually seasick middy.

The *cuberta* they had lugged in tow from Manaos was brought up, and James and William and two hands

153

scrambled down into it. The whole thing was tending towards the absurd, James thought, but the *cuberta* was necessary in case there was rubber ashore that Baines would not want to know about but which James would insist on transferring to the *Neptune*. Baines' eyes were at this moment no doubt firmly fixed on the *Lago Grande*, that huge inland sea which stretched in the other direction. James wondered if Baines would in fact persevere in his determination to leave the sea once he had got back to England. Seated for'ard of the narrow *cuberta* deck, William still tried to shake off his illness as they made their way towards the distant landing place.

There was no sign of life as they tied up and went ashore. The jungle began almost immediately here, well-defined tracks cut through it at certain points. It was safe enough to proceed as long as one did not stray from these 'highways'. Baines had walked this way when he came ashore to find Henriques, and so had Lombardo on another occasion. But it was all new to James.

It was a good couple of miles to the house with its suspicious surround of rush mats and stakes driven into the ground. It was a long, low and mean house, that would hardly have been attractive even if its tiled roof had been in good repair and the verandah had not been falling down. Heavy chains, rusted from humid exposure, dangled from the crude stakes. The place gave every appearance of having been deserted for some time.

James looked around and sighed. The shadows were beginning to draw in. The unseen hand would draw the velvet curtain if they were not brisk, and it was not the sort of place to be caught in the dark. 'Naught here then,' commented James to William.

'What did this Senhor Henriques or whatever his name is do here, Uncle James?' asked William, his eyes flickering over the stakes and chains. 'Was he . . . well, I've heard that slavery still goes on in this country, I mean, but did Henriques – '

'None of our business that, lad,' cut in James, quickly turning his back on the troubling scene. 'Where's the rubber, that's what I want to know. There's got to be some about here. He can't have spirited all away in a trice, his goods and carts and . . . and whatever else he kept here.'

James' eye suddenly fell on a kind of roughly constructed shed deeper in the trees. It was almost invisible because of the density of the jungle surrounding it: in fact, if James had not been standing precisely where he was in the clearing, he would not have seen it.

'Wait here,' said James to William.

'Where are you going?'

'Never mind. Just wait.'

He did not know why he found it necessary to approach the shed silently and with care. Plainly it could not be inhabited. It was most probably entirely empty. But James made as little sound as possible moving up to the door of the place. He was out of sight of William and the two hands when he finally stood before it. The shadows were longer.

James very gently eased open the rickety door. Inside was a great mound of raw rubber, at least three times as much as he was accustomed to collect from any of his agents. Henriques must obviously have had warning of the visit of the police, and found time enough to conceal his spoils.

James opened his mouth to shout joyfully to William and the hands, but before he could utter a word a voice abruptly whispered at his left ear: 'So, Senhor Capitao. You wish this rubber? But other business come first. Other business.'

James swung his head into the gloom of the shed. Something stirred in the darkness, someone leapt at him. Then it was as though his head exploded. A fury of blazing lights burst over him, and for a time he knew no more.

When James Onedin regained his senses, it was to find himself lying on the ground staring up, far up, into the black tops of giant trees. All around him it was deep night, but pale light proceeded from a strange flickering source, suspended above and to the right of him. James groaned, only aware that he had been hit on the head with something and that his head ached outrageously. It became obvious after a little that the light was a storm lantern hanging from the lower branch of a tree. Then he saw a negro with a rifle leaning against the tree trunk.

Seeing James stir, the negro turned and called something in Portuguese into the night. There was a pause, and then a tall man smoking a cigar came into the circle of light. He stopped, staring judiciously down at James. It was Henriques.

James blinked at him. He tried to sit up, but his head throbbed. 'Henriques . . . ' he breathed. 'What – what the devil . . . Was it you . . . why . . . ' Memory flooded back. 'My nephew,' he exclaimed. 'Young William. What's happened to him? And the hands from the *Neptune* . . . ?'

'Do not fear.' Henriques' tone was curt. The broken English, which before had made his speech a kind of singsong, now made it brisk and metallic. 'Other peoples, Henriques he not bringing this place. Only you. Other peoples, they going back ship. One of my men, he hit you. Maybe too hard. I sorry. But you having rubber now. I give.'

James was utterly bewildered. It all seemed too extraordinary. Certainly he had been brought to some other place: the jungle around him, in as much as he could make it out, was not the jungle of the land close to the river. And the house in the clearing was nowhere to be seen. 'You – you want to *give* me that rubber?' he asked feebly. 'Why?'

'You take. You having this much. Now you give Henriques plenty. You see.' He rapped something at the negro against the tree, who came forward and unceremoniously hauled James to his feet. James staggered, so weak he felt he must simply collapse again, but his powerful captor thrust his arm up behind his back, propelling him forward with one hand while he still clutched his rifle with the other.

They stumbled through coarse undergrowth, Henriques following. A sound of sobbing began to reach them, isolated, eerie in the black bush. The negro halted and shouted something angry into the darkness. The sobbing ceased. The still only partly-conscious James thought he perceived an uneasy stirring, as of a number of frightened people. There was an identifiable clanking of metal. The negro drove James on.

Light glowed ahead again, and in a little they moved into another glimmering circle. Here a stout little individual who looked to be a *mameluco* held a rifle, and a storm lantern again hung from one of the Amazonian giants. The tree seemed so broad and so huge that it was all there was to be seen. It was reared up on roots, themselves the thickness of European trees, that had burst up out of the ground, forming a vast dark chamber beneath.

Henriques lit yet another storm lantern, and entered the chamber beneath the tree. The negro forced a now confused and apprehensive James after him, clutching his arm tighter than ever.

But no premonition of evil could have prepared James for what met his eyes in the white gleam of the lamp. He perhaps feared that further harm was intended to himself. What he saw was three persons, three women, in ragged and grubby clothes, tied with thick bands to projecting sections of upraised roots. The light of the lamp appeared to dazzle them, so that they could at first see nothing. The woman in the centre, plainly younger than the others, had been crying. She was Charlotte, and the other two were Letty and Elizabeth.

James gaped. A cry, something closer to a yell perhaps,

leapt to his lips. He could only stare, petrified. Henriques turned black eyes on him.

'So, Capitao,' he hissed. 'English ladies. Henriques, he saving English ladies from Indians, who wish them much harm. English ladies live because Henriques is kind man. But now, Capitao, Henriques must have money for them.'

'Papa!' Charlotte was sobbing, having made out who it was, equally unable to believe in anything. 'Don't listen to him. The Indians helped us. But he is a slaver. He's taken the Indians captive.'

'What is the meaning of this?' James found his voice suddenly. 'Let them go! Let them go this minute!'

'They will not be safe, Senhor Capitao.' Henriques flashed one of his white smiles at James. 'The Indians, they will kill them. And Henriques must have reward for saving ladies.'

'Let them go, I say! Untie their arms!' James wrenched violently, but could not get away from the powerful negro. He swung around, attempting to smash a fist in the man's face, but the other at once brought the rifle he held heavily down on James' arm. James cried out in pain. Spurts of fire shot up his arm.

'We can't fight them, James! Do as they say!' It was Elizabeth calling to him. Elizabeth, gaunt from her privations, at the end of her resources, a person he did not remember.

His arm numbed with the hurt of the blow, James again stared at the Onedin women before him. Elizabeth seemed in fact only half conscious. Charlotte wept in misery and bitter fear. Letty merely met her husband's gaze, unable to speak, hollow-cheeked, bleak, suppliant.

A bandage was rudely pulled around James' eyes, blotting out the unhappy women and the whole violent scene from his sight. Again a voice whispered in his ear.

'So, Capitao. You rich man now. You having much

158

money. You go back ship. My men take you. One week today, you come landing place. You not bring other peoples. You have for Henriques fifty million *reis*. Or your English ladies ... I fear very much Indians kill them.'

CHAPTER ELEVEN

'Fifty million *reis*,' cried James in a transport of despair. 'Good God above, that's nearly fifty thousand pounds.'

'And you're to take it to the devil? Just like that?' Baines was overwhelmed by the enormity of it too. Both kidnapping and huge sums of money were to a person of his station matters of complete unreality.

'He'll be at the landing place – ' James looked quickly at the calendar on the wall of the dock office – 'this Thursday. I'm to be back there this Thursday with fifty million *reis*. He gave me no more than a week.'

'You'll have to call in the authorities,' grunted Baines. 'They're not much use here, not like British peelers, but you'll have to take what help they can give.'

'Do we have any guarantee,' asked William, who stood staring out the office window, 'that if the money is paid over, my mother and the other women will actually be freed?'

James could have done perfectly well without William at this particular time. He still protested he felt ill, and indeed looked distinctly poorly. But concern for his mother would not allow him to rest or seek medical advice. James found his constant presence depressing.

Yet William had also been duly concerned for his uncle back at the landing place. James was forced to admit that. After being shown the captive women in the tree chamber, James had been propelled blindfold through the jungle by Henriques' men, over a distance that he could not gauge but which had seemed to take a singularly long time to traverse. Then he had all at once been thrust rudely ahead of them, so violently that he fell. The men had thereupon vanished into the morass of green which they obviously knew as well as other men know towns.

James knew instinctively he was back at the house in the clearing. He called out loudly and repeatedly, and after a little time it was William who came to his rescue. William, who had remained ashore all night, braving the dangers of the place because he did not know what had happened to his uncle and wished to be of service to him should he return. As he untied James and released the bandage over his eyes, William had been seized by a little spasm that could have been fever.

Baines had naturally not wished to persevere with his voyage to England once he heard about the women. 'Young Miss Charlotte?' he had echoed in astonishment and anger. 'Mrs Onedin and Lady Fogarty? Good God, sir, let's get ashore and whip these filthy curs while we may.'

But it had been decided on balance that this would not be the wisest plan. The jungle would certainly do for them even if Henriques and his minions with their rifles did not. They were totally unarmed. There seemed no choice therefore but to return to Manaos and assess the situation comprehensively. And such cold and dispassionate assessment had in the end left them with but one conclusion.

'I think we can be sure the captives will be freed if the money's paid over,' said James in reply to William at the window of the dock office. 'But there would certainly be trouble if we tried to involve the authorities. I can't see Henriques stopping short at murder. Yet fifty million *reis* . . . ! Dear heaven, how shall I lay my hands on a sum like that?'

'Surely you have the likes of fifty thousand pounds to your name, sir.' Baines was deliberately blunt. He had no intention of enduring James' familiar moan about money under the present circumstances.

'I'd need to have more than that,' responded James in a hard voice, unwilling to discuss it. 'The amount I lost over Port Baines would finance a small state. Where's Lombardo, for pity's sake? Does he have to be away just at the time I need him?'

'He's upriver. After rubber again.'

'Fifty thousand pounds will make a great hole in my profits from rubber,' pronounced James. The tone was tart now. 'Is there absolutely no other way of freeing Letty and the others?'

'Good God, sir, you'd think in a fashion like that with your wife and child and sister held by a slaver?' Baines was outraged.

'Spending capital for any reason is throwing the future away,' James informed him brusquely. 'And there's no need to talk of slavers. Henriques must have known of the healthy state of my business and seen an opportunity to make a fortune for himself out of kidnap and blackmail. It's naught to do with slaving.'

'Rubber profits is to do with slaving,' rejoined Baines. 'And profits such as you've made out of rubber you're now complaining you've got to hand back to one of the ones who forced men to work unpaid. Sounds like a waste of time all round.'

'Uncle James,' said William in a curiously shaky voice. 'You must do nothing to endanger my mother's life.'

'Why have you come to join her like this, anyway?' James shot the question at him. 'Am I never to hear the truth of that?' It seemed as good a time as any to raise the question. Yet the boy, framed by the window with the docks beyond, seemed now to be swaying visibly. 'What the blue blazes is the matter with you? Are you sick or aren't you? And will you not dig out some sawbones and see what he's got to say?' James' voice cracked round the office. He had decided he had had just about enough of young William.

William seemed to smile faintly. Yet it was a meaningless smile, for nothing had been said either to please or amuse him. All at once his legs buckled and he slid gently to the floor.

Baines was at his side in a minute. 'He's red hot, sir!' he exclaimed, feeling the young man's head. 'Hot as coals!'

'Then he'll have to be got to bed.' James allowed himself to be secretly pleased. That was William out of his hair. Fevers came and fevers went, and were useful betimes. It was all in the head. James remembered how years previously he had lain in his master's berth ravaged with violent shivers, sweat pouring out of him as his ship had rounded the Cape. Twelve hours later, quite tired of all that, he had been on his feet on the poop in a howling gale, roaring orders to the hands above, revelling in the tempest. 'There's the new ward they've opened in the hospital that was only finished last year. Doubtless they'll take him in and care for him until he's restored to health ... '

Charlotte peered out through the interstices of the gigantic roots. Creeper and foliage had grown here, so that it was like looking through irregular trellis-work. Charlotte felt herself to be sticky and grubby, but she was as alert as the morning itself. The sad column marched by outside: Indians, perhaps forty of them, being led away to work on the rubber trees. Henriques had been roaming the district, assembling another work team. On his black horse, he cracked a whip over his slaves' heads. They were chained together so that Henriques needed only two overseers to govern the group. One of the overseers was the big negro.

Charlotte looked back into the tree chamber that was their prison. Elizabeth still lay against the root she was secured to, listless and defeated. Charlotte wondered if she were perhaps very ill. Letty was more awake, but hardly communicative. Further over the *mameluco* who guarded them was mixing up the *pirarucu* he had been ordered to give the women for their food. This was an almost edible mess of beans and bacon. He was occupied, paying no attention to anything else. It occurred to Charlotte that while Henriques and the overseers took the Indians to their forced labour, this man would be the only one left in charge of them.

'Charlotte,' asked Letty without preamble in a dull voice. 'Do you think I hate you . . . ?'

The girl was considerably startled. The morning sun fell through the trees outside, making arbitrary patterns of light, so that in the tree chamber it was for once not so gloomy. Letty seemed as it were abstracted from their condition. Her expression was reflective and a little sad.

Charlotte was unable to think of a reply, and Letty looked quickly to her. 'Oh, I don't mean you *shouldn't* think that,' she went on with the ghost of a smile. 'In fact it would surprise me very much if you had come to any other conclusion. In a sense, you see . . . it's true.'

Now Charlotte was bewildered. She could not imagine why her stepmother was talking to her in this manner. 'Letty,' she began nervously, 'perhaps – '

'Resentment.' Letty settled back in her bonds. She was easing her pain, but for a moment it was almost as though she were an aged and venerable lady settling in a favourite chair. How old was Letty anyway? Charlotte could not tell why she invariably thought of Letty as older than her father. 'Resentment,' her stepmother went on. 'It was always *your* life, you know. Charlotte, *your* concerns. Before I married your father, afterwards. In fact I think the only real reason he married me was to assure himself there

164

would be someone to care for you. Was I a fool? Was it idiocy on my part to think all that only for a time? That sooner or later . . . I would make James Onedin love me?

'Yet as I grew older and more set in my ways, you emerged into young womanhood. As I grew tired, you grew livelier. As the lines deepened and pitted on my face . . . you grew beautiful.'

Letty lowered her eyes, sombre and very still for a moment. She knew now she was jealous of Charlotte. It seemed to her James had sensed that too. Of course James had neglected her. Of course he had always taken her for granted. But that did not obliterate the fact that she had wasted her energies in a stupid and powerful misdirection. Was what had happened to the women some kind of vengeance from on high for her pettiness? She had given in to a silly passion that would have disgraced a schoolgirl. She felt ashamed.

'I need to say . . . I'm sorry, Charlotte,' Letty continued in a low voice. 'Your father will do everything in his power to rescue you, you don't have to worry. But I wouldn't blame him if he did nothing to rescue me. Where's my value to him? I've let him down. I've betrayed him by seeking to reduce him to what I am. I've asked him to be half the human person he is.'

The *mameluco* came over with the food. As he knelt with the wooden bowl to ladle some of the *pirarucu* out for each, Charlotte looked him straight in the eye. She was unable to work out completely what Letty was saying to her, but it had been occurring to her that this man must understand very clearly what *she* felt. 'Why are you doing this?' she asked bluntly in a tongue she knew the *mameluco* must comprehend. 'You, with the blood of the Indian people in your veins. You work for this villain. An oppressor. A rogue who takes your brothers and sisters captive . . . '

The *mameluco* ignored her words. There was a sudden resounding clang not far away, an inexplicable sound almost like iron hitting something hollow and resonating. The *mameluco* looked up quickly. Oddly, the morning light seemed to have dimmed. A cloud had passed over the sun. It was gloomy in the jungle once more.

'Why don't you let us go?' demanded Charlotte. 'Cut our bonds with that knife. Set us free.'

Again there was the strange resounding clang out in the gloom. 'What on earth is that noise?' asked Letty wearily. 'I heard it last night. I was trying to sleep and it kept waking me up.'

'It's a jungle noise,' Charlotte replied. 'I've read about it. An echoing sound that lots of people seem to hear in the Amazon, but that nobody's ever been able to explain. The Indians say . . . ' She broke off, looking to the *mameluco* again. His face wore a deep frown as he served out the food. Each captive had one hand free to take up and consume the food, and the *mameluco* was placing an individual dish before each of them in turn.

'You're all alone here now, aren't you?' said Charlotte quietly in the native tongue. 'You don't care about us. Why should you? But you ought to care about yourself. You, with the blood of Indians in your veins. The *Mauhes*, perhaps. Or the *Mundurucu* themselves . . . those great warriors . . . '

Charlotte allowed her eyes to drift to the sombre world outside the tree chamber. As though commanded to it, the resounding clang occurred again. This time it seemed closer, and the *mameluco* stiffened. 'You know what I think that is?' the English girl enquired of him. 'I think that is what my mother told me it was when I was only a baby. I think that is . . . the *curupira* . . . '

The *mameluco*'s jaw dropped. His eyes were on as much as he could see of the tall forest from their prison. 'No good sheltering in the trees,' Charlotte said bleakly. 'The *curupira* rules all the trees. All that can save even the bravest man from the *curupira* is water. The *curupira* won't cross water.'

166

So a wise man won't stay alone ... he'll run hard to a stream ... get over it ...'

The resounding clang echoed all about them. The *mameluco* gave a sudden yell and leapt up, racing out of the tree chamber. He was still yelling as he vanished into the trees in the direction opposite to that from which the sound had proceeded. Elizabeth at once strained for the knife he had been using, but could not quite reach it. 'Aunt Elizabeth,' she urged. 'Aunt Elizabeth! You get the knife.'

Elizabeth roused from the odd lethargy that she seemed to have fallen into. 'What ... Charlotte ...'

'The knife! The knife, Aunt Elizabeth!'

Elizabeth picked up the knife rather stupidly and handed it to Charlotte. The girl began at once to saw at her bonds.

Letty was bewildered. 'What happened, Charlotte?' she enquired. 'And what *is* that sound?'

'Oh, the Indians have an old myth about the spirit of the forest,' Charlotte replied as she ripped at the rope. 'He's a sort of a wild man with cloven feet and a bright red face. Not the least bit friendly. So they give him a wide berth.' One strand of the hawser-like material they had been tied up with snapped apart. 'It'd be funny if that *was* the truth about that banging sound, though, wouldn't it?' she queried. 'We'd be out of the frying pan into the fire ...'

Letty appreciated she was in the presence of James Onedin's daughter: James without the blindness, the stubbornness, the dogged materialism. And she had been stupid enough to believe she hated her.

When Daniel Fogarty walked into the dock office at Manaos, James Onedin believed he was at last losing his grip on reality. It was out of all conscience. He and his family might as well have been back in Birkenhead, inviting each other to Sunday luncheon.

'What the devil –' was all he could manage.

167

'What's all this about Elizabeth?' rapped Daniel. 'I heard from your man Lombardo her ship had been stolen from her and her whereabouts weren't known. Now I hear you know where she is, and she's in trouble.'

'How do you hear that?' James was bemused by the rush of events.

'I ran into Baines. He was astonished to see me too. I tried to find you as soon as I knew about Elizabeth, but you weren't in the city. Somewhere downriver, they said.'

'What in heaven's name are you doing in a place like Manaos, man – ?'

Daniel paused. *You may well ask*, he thought to himself sombrely. In fact he was no longer very sure why he was there either. Learning that Elizabeth was in trouble somehow had put a different complexion on things. Daniel could not say why: at the height of his infatuation with Chiara Santa he had thought everything between him and his wife quite finished. Infatuation. There, he had said it. Chiara was to sing that night: the great *musicale* was to be held and virtually all Manaos would attend; yet Daniel now did not wish to be involved. It was disconcerting, and in a sense mysterious.

'I understand you're in financial difficulties,' said Daniel bluntly to James.

James eyed him. But there was no point in dissimulation. 'Aye,' he muttered, 'and what's become of Elizabeth and Letty and young Charlotte will compound those difficulties.' And he told Daniel as much as he knew of the piracy and the kidnapping of the women.

Daniel was utterly aghast. 'Fifty thousand pounds!' he exclaimed. 'And you're going to give it to this criminal Henriques?'

'I'm raising it,' rejoined James, his tone distinctly warm as he regarded the other. 'But as you may appreciate, in financial difficulties that isn't easy.' .

'Don't be absurd. If the sum is to be paid over, naturally

168

I have funds to cover it. But what I'm asking is, are you and I – are *we* – going to meet it?'

James blinked. 'I don't see we've any choice.' He found himself looking at Daniel Fogarty in a new light. It was a long time since they had behaved towards each other with anything other than veiled hostility, but now they were men facing precisely the same problem. There was a crisis involving their loved ones. They were men with a common purpose. 'If we give Henriques half a chance, he'll kill the women.'

'They're being held somewhere deep in the jungle, you say,' mused Daniel. 'What sort of a journey though? How long?'

'God knows. It seemed to me when I was blindfolded I was dragged over some kind of path for a couple of hours.'

'Path? It was a path?'

'A jungle path! That means it's just a way through the underbush and trees. Known only to a few. Others would perish trying to follow it.'

'Others except those who know how to follow such a path.' Daniel nodded thoughtfully. Then he looked sharply to his companion. 'James Onedin, you're getting slack. Tropical indolence is taking its toll of you. There was a time when you would never have submitted to demands like those being made on you at this moment. Never mind if they came from criminal, bank manager or fellow seafarer.' He grinned tautly, recalling their past tussles with grim pleasure. He saw Elizabeth's face: Elizabeth when James had forcibly separated him from her, and driven her into Albert Frazer's arms. 'You see to yourself. You are knocked down only to get up again. You disappoint me, James. I respected you almost as much as I despised you in times gone by. You may have been my foe, but you were also my mentor.'

'What are you saying we should do, man?' James could not follow Daniel, though his words sounded ringing echoes within him. He had indeed declined in this place. Money

169

alone and the pursuit of money had ruled him. Over this last and most tearing demand on him, he had even perhaps become the sort of person he had once looked down on. 'We can't fight when it's others who may be harmed.'

'We can fight,' replied Daniel Fogarty. The young Elizabeth would no doubt have approved of the fact that when, aboard the river steamer, Chiara Santa had left her cabin door ajar for Daniel, he had for some reason or other found himself unable to enter. He had gone there by dead of night, knowing she would be waiting for him, and at the last minute had turned away. He had not then for the life of him known why, and perhaps knew only very obscurely even now. 'We can fight,' repeated Daniel. 'As long as we fight by your self-centred rules . . .'

The *Neptune* had a proud beauty as she prepared to cast off. The day was muggy, as most days seemed to be in these latitudes, but there was still wind enough to fill the sails, and the regular steamer moored further along at the pontoon looked positively grey and ignoble by comparison. James wondered irrelevantly if he chased an impossible dream where shipping was concerned. Even in the construction of the ill-fated Port Baines he had had to allow for the fact that he would inevitably be concerned more with steamships than with sailing vessels: a development that had in fact never been begun was the establishing of an efficient coal bunker. Yet were the white ships to be permitted to moulder in dank ports, banned forever from the blue seas? It seemed a wretched end to soaring spars, sturdy sea walls.

'Awaiting your order, Captain Onedin, sir.' Baines tipped a salute in which there was no longer any servility. He had expanded when he had learned James and the newly arrived Daniel Fogarty were going to fight for their women. Arms had been taken aboard the *Neptune*, and Baines walked the deck as square-jawed and grim-faced as if he had been commanding a man-o'-war and a contingent of marines.

James nodded. He in his turn was awaiting Daniel, whom he had had also to tell of his son William and the fever that had felled him. Daniel had gone quickly to the hospital. 'I might have guessed he was here,' had been his flat comment on his son's presence in Manaos. 'In search of his mother, of course. Because he thought I was betraying her. And him too. Him too.'

James' eyes drifted across the deck. A little group squatted there, waiting. There were three of them, and they were *caboclos*, the city Indians who spoke the white man's tongue and lived the white man's life. But they were not entirely ignorant of the traditional Indian skills. Baines had found these three who could help materially with the current enterprise. James again felt the acute irony of his continuing relationship with these native people of the continent. They always seemed to be coming to the aid of him and his dependents in some way, and in return he treated them only with a kind of contempt. He had profited grossly from their labour. In all but name he had enslaved them.

'There's Captain Fogarty, sir.' Baines still gave Daniel his nautical title. Any other title he might have acquired was on this deck secondary and unimportant. As Daniel came aboard, Baines roared 'Lay aloft' above him, and the gangway was drawn up and the lines cast off. But Daniel's face was grave.

'Young William,' he announced to James. 'They say it's yellow fever . . . '

'My God . . . '

'We have other things to do. Everything's being done for him as possibly can be.' Daniel shook his head to drive away the worry of it. Yellow fever (as his wife had discovered, could he but have known it) remained the tropical killer. As leprosy itself once stalked Europe, so here the disease that turned men a drained and jaundiced colour took its persistent toll.

A little tug nosed at the *Neptune*, shoving her out into stream. Soon she would spread her wings. 'A pity Lombardo isn't back from his trip yet,' said James to make conversation, for the furrows were deep in Daniel's brow.

'Lombardo – ?'

James chuckled. 'He must have got held up longer than he expected. Must be cursing himself at this moment for not ensuring he got back earlier. Well, he's mad on music and opera,' he grinned as Daniel looked perplexed, 'and that Italian singer's to appear tonight. Clara – Chiara – '

Daniel did not bother to complete the name for him. The furrows in his brow deepened. 'We have other things to do, James. Art, mortal illness, any other consideration you can think of . . . nothing whatever must detain us.'

CHAPTER TWELVE

'Wait,' gasped Elizabeth, supporting herself against a tree a moment. 'Wait . . . '

'Aunt Elizabeth, we must press on!' Only pale light dripped down through the utterly enclosing jungle here, and Charlotte's face was curiously hard to distinguish. But Elizabeth needed no blazing torch to tell her it was drawn with anxiety. They seemed to be in a world where rampant growth got ever denser, where the earth and sky equally were concealed and movement more than a foot in any direction was impossible. It was a world into which Charlotte had led them.

'I must rest,' moaned Elizabeth. 'Rest.'

'Come dear,' said Letty, putting an arm around her to support her. 'It's all right. I'll help you.'

That seemed odd, the bemused Elizabeth thought. She was at the end of her tether, and it was Letty of all people who seemed to be helping her. Elizabeth did not know what was the matter with her. She did not think she was ill. When Charlotte had released her in the tree chamber and it had become plain to her that an escape from their captors was possible, she had responded with alacrity. But the recovery was short-lived. She really was abominably tired, having borne the major responsibility for the party since they had left Santos on the *Lady Elizabeth* so long ago and then entered into their arduous adventures. The three had only gone a few miles into the jungle when Elizabeth again felt weak and became a burden on the other two.

Charlotte was convinced that she knew the way to the river. There was no established track, nor even any certainty of direction, but the young woman maintained she had learned from the Indians long ago the manner of following a path in the jungle. 'You have to keep a sharp eye,' she told Elizabeth with a girlish confidence that in the circumstances was hardly reassuring. 'Twigs and small branches are bent in a certain way where people have passed. There can be marks underfoot. As long as you know what to look for, you can't go wrong. I learned all about it at Port Baines. The Indians there taught me so much.'

But still not enough, thought Elizabeth bleakly. Still not enough. They were in a dense enveloping maze where it would have been impossible to notice any so-called signs even if they had been there. They had obviously been fools to fall in with Charlotte's notions. If their captors did not now catch up with them again, they must surely die. And Letty, Letty of all people, was calm and even sanguine. It made no sense.

'Look,' said Letty, suddenly pointing. 'Look there.'

They were in a green cathedral, Elizabeth decided drowsily. She wished she could sleep for a very long time. A green cathedral stretching high above. If you listened you could hear the choir. Or was that those ridiculous yelping birds again – ? Why then were they singing, quite clearly, *Day of wrath, O day of mourning . . . ?*

She came to her senses sharply. 'Yes!' Charlotte was crying joyfully. 'Yes, Letty, you're right. It's a footprint. The clearest we've seen yet!'

'I thought it must be from the way the scrub bent down into the little hollow,' responded Letty. 'It's the sort of

174

thing you've been looking for all day, dear.'

Despite the grime and little cuts from the foliage on her face, Charlotte was radiant. 'I'd never have seen it, Letty. Not here. Now wait a moment. It means the track goes – this way, doesn't it? That's right. This is obviously just a difficult section. Once we're out of the thick stuff ...'

Letty and Charlotte seem to be getting on rather better, thought Elizabeth vaguely as Letty came once more to her aid, assisting her. It really is remarkable. You tell yourself people won't be able to stand up to hardship, and they turn out to be the most resilient ones of all ...

Chiara Santa was to sing in the salon of the fine government building that was by day the offices of the Amazonas Province. She had spent the afternoon rehearsing with the pianist supplied to her, reducing him to tears with her rendering of *Madre, pietosa vergine* from *La Forza del Destino*. But Chiara, worried as to where Daniel might be – he had said he would lunch with her and had then not arrived – knew she had been flat on her final top A. She tried the phrase again, and made the same error. When later, having rehearsed something else, she came back to *Madre, pietosa vergine,* she was still flat. Chiara supposed it was nerves. And a kind of concern. She had left the door to her cabin ajar on the last night on the river steamer. But Daniel had not come to her. Why?

She went back to her hotel to rest, wash and change. Still there was no word from Daniel. Chiara found herself a little put out. The town whole-heartedly adored her. Everywhere people bowed, dropped curtsies, or kissed her hand at the least excuse. But Daniel had not come to her cabin, although she had been certain at one point during the night that he had been in the corridor just outside. Why had he gone away again? Had the goddess refused him entry?

She lay down for a little, and as her eyelids dropped it

occurred to Chiara Santa that it could be said she had not been truly listening for the goddess' voice of late. Here in this extraordinary, extravagant, utterly unlikely city in the heart of the jungle, she was abandoned to unreality. It was, as Daniel had said, a state of 'life between'. All of it. Daniel's smile haunted the darkness behind her eyes. He was a genuinely handsome man, the sort that most women would feel themselves flattered to have attracted. Well, there were hotel bedroom doors that could be left ajar, Chiara reflected.

As she dressed, she was expecting Daniel to knock at any time. But when a knock finally did come it was the manager of the concert, plump and beaming in his tails, to escort her to her performance. The salon was just across the road from her hotel.

Down in the lobby, the admirers were all gathered, armed with flowers and obeisances. But of Daniel, no sign whatever. Annoyance turned to hurt in Chiara, for he could surely not have been injured. Of that she would have heard. He was therefore staying away deliberately. What sort of a man was he? The concert manager was backing away before her, making repeated and adulatory bows. Chiara bore him no ill will, but would heartily have liked him to back down an open trap and vanish.

The applause in the salon as she appeared was thunderous. Daniel wanted to humiliate her, that was what it was. He had allowed himself to be seen with her as her companion, and now he was purposely not attending her performance. As she smiled and bowed, her eyes raked the lacquered and gilded chairs that had been set out for the splendidly attired audience. Surely he was there somewhere. Coming in late, exhausted, repentant – ?

Chiara Santa began to sing. She was not in the best possible voice, it came to her as she commenced. The dazzled audience appeared to notice nothing, but she and the goddess knew. Chiara became a little troubled as she trilled on. Perhaps the goddess was angry at her over her bland selection

176

of Daniel? She had certainly never said to him that any relationship must be on *her* terms. The goddess could be jealous, that she knew. She remembered her first teacher of singing, years previously. His injunction had been that she was entering into the service of the most difficult and capricious mistress known to man. Let her beware. Violetta failed to take proper care in *La Traviata*, and look what happened to her.

Caro nome was greeted rapturously. Chiara was encouraged. She did not need Daniel there. Of course not. She needed no man unless of the kind of which the goddess completely approved. As her voice soared up in *Madre, pietosa vergine* she understood she was going to have a triumph. It was scintillating. It was brilliant. There remained only the top A. And on it, she was suddenly, horrifyingly flat.

It was absurd, of course. She had hit top A before with ease. She could manage the C above it if necessary. What then was wrong? The audience stirred minimally. Some had noticed. *Ah, che la morte!* She sang the reprise with a rare sweetness, to distract those who had noted the imprecision. But inevitably the top A came again.

This time she missed it by at least a semitone. The stirring of the audience was considerably louder, and Chiara was shaken. She had never known herself to sing with such laxity. She had never dreamed such a disaster could be laid at her door.

It was the end. It was ruin. Quite clearly, the gift of the goddess was being taken away from her, because the goddess was outraged and savagely angry at her for leaving her cabin door unlocked to Daniel Fogarty, from whom she had only saved her worthless client by direct intervention. And Chiara had not realised! *Parmi veder le lagrime! O terra, addio!*

'We'll go no further,' ordered James quietly. 'We'll lay to

here. If Senhor Henriques has left a patrol to spy on the landing place, he won't want to be warned we're coming in force.'

Baines nodded briefly. It was getting towards nightfall, and they were to go ashore as secretly as possible. The party consisted of himself, James, Daniel Fogarty and two seamen who had volunteered, together with the Indians. They really should have travelled by *cuberta*, which would have aroused less suspicion on the river. But there had never been any question but that they should carry out this mission with the aid of the splendid *Neptune*. Baines had found that fitting.

They lowered a ship's boat and rowed ashore. It was quiet, and they were approaching a deserted spot. But an alligator slid into the water as they approached, startling them.

'My God,' muttered Baines. He did not care for these denizens of the deep which were neither proper sea monsters nor dolphins that could make you laugh, leaping in and out of the water beside your ship through many a long sea mile.

'What if William dies?' It was the worried whisper of Daniel, next to James.

'Don't be stupid. Don't talk like that.'

'If William dies, it will be the hardest thing I have ever been called upon to bear,' Daniel's whisper went on. 'But I know now, as I have not known before, that if Elizabeth dies . . . why, that will be worse still. That will be the end of me.'

James frowned deeply. He wondered if he could say something the same, deep in his heart. If Charlotte dies . . . if Letty dies . . . He preferred to put the whole matter from his mind. He was doing what he was doing so that nobody should die.

They got ashore while enough light remained. The Indians, able to read the jungle signs, were to take them inland from this point, turning upstream until they came to the clearing and Henriques' house, and then identifying for them the path that James had been led over blindfold. The party hoped that surprise would give them the advantage, and they had a carefully worked out plan of attack that would avoid the taking of life. But, as Baines had observed grimly, 'that devil's armed, and we'd be less than men to stand by and be shot by a devil like that.'

It was not an arduous trip through this coastal section of the jungle. As night finally came down James called a halt, and they lay down on the ground to rest briefly. They would move again at the first glimmer of light. The jungle was full of sound, and James dozed only fitfully. It was like being at sea when some danger threatened but would not reveal itself. The face that came constantly into his mind through these half-wakeful periods of sleep was not Charlotte's, as he might have expected, but Letty's. At sea when great danger threatened but would not reveal itself, the face in sleep had always been Anne's.

As dawn came up fully, Charlotte, Letty and Elizabeth (still supported for the most part by Letty) found their way to a jungle stream. They had heard the run of the water where they had had to pause for the night, and as the first grey slivers of day probed their way down through the trees, moved towards it. They simply fell down at the stream and let their heads droop into it. They had had no food now for well over a day, and before that had in no sense been well fed. They were hungry, thirsty, weary and abominably grubby.

After a little Charlotte lifted her head out of the cool, cleansing water. 'Shall we look for food?' she asked in a dead voice. 'There must be something . . . '

'How much further have we to go?' Letty responded to her question with another. 'I get the impression we've been going in circles . . . ' Charlotte appreciated that it had been a prodigious strain on Letty dragging Elizabeth along. But Letty had accepted – almost dutifully, her stepdaughter thought wryly – that Charlotte was the pathfinder, and that therefore Charlotte must be freed for the concentration her task required. I am being shown another side of Letty, pondered Charlotte. It is a side that a little while ago I would have said did not exist. 'How will it be when we finally reach the river? We may come to a barren place. Where there's nothing.'

'Father will come back to the place where he's to meet Henriques. He must. I'm hoping this path will lead us direct to him.'

'Do you think your father will spend fifty million *reis* on us?' asked Letty in immense weariness. She felt now as tired as Elizabeth looked. 'That's almost – ' She could not compute. She gave a fatigued gesture. 'Won't he think better of throwing away such a sum of money?'

'Letty.'

'You need to get something back for such an investment. He gets you back, of course – but he also has to take me . . . ' Letty was speaking very directly to her stepdaughter now, one woman addressing another. 'I was foolish, Charlotte. Very foolish indeed not to see that his affection for you did not in any way conflict with his affection for me. He is not a man to show emotion, of course, but I see now he did offer me the love of which he was capable. For all practical purposes, I told him it was not enough. I told him I would have love of another sort, or I would do without love. I blamed him for loving you. He – and you – must have been very confused.'

There were bright tears in Charlotte's eyes as she regarded the other woman, not entirely the result of overstrain and tiredness. 'Don't you know I've always loved you as far as it was possible, Letty? You weren't my mama, and I knew it. But that didn't mean I wasn't grateful to you for what you were doing. That I didn't need you. Perhaps I'm too like

180

Papa. Not able to show emotion properly.'

'Child, child.' Moved too, Letty reached out a hand to grasp Charlotte's.

'Letty. Forgive me.'

'My dearest Charlotte.'

'Good morning, English ladies,' said a soft voice behind them. 'I much hope you sleep good.'

Letty swung her head round, and Charlotte gasped loudly. Henriques stood at the nearest tree, rifle in hand, his white teeth gleaming in a smile. The negro was behind him, and then two other armed men the women had not seen before. Henriques beamed ingratiatingly. 'It is hard to journey in the jungle,' he smiled. 'People are dying sometimes. You must know path very good.' His grin broadened. 'But you have most good luck, English ladies. You do not meet *curupira*.'

He laughed loud and long, and the sound of it echoed back from the tall, comfortless trees.

The leading *caboclo* indicated the way. James was made humble by the manner in which they could observe for a long and intense moment, decide on direction with complete certainty, then move through even the thickest jungle as noiselessly as a cat. White men could not do that. White men had other skills and thought themselves superior. But were these skills any the less? James had once brought the white man's skills to this land, most of all with his fine bridge that spanned the gorge at Port Baines and which now lay in an ignoble, rusting heap at the bottom of the ravine. Would Indian skills ever have been so inept, so brash and misguided?

'By God, sir!' It was Baines. The leading *caboclo* had stopped dead, pointing ahead. Through a little break in the trees, persons were suddenly visible. They were proceeding along a jungle path, wide enough to be recognisable at this point, apparently quite unaware they were observed. They were four armed men, one of whom was a negro, another Henriques; then Letty and Charlotte Onedin supporting between them Elizabeth Fogarty.

'Elizabeth – !' It was the merest shocked whisper, but Daniel Fogarty was shaken by the sight of his wife. He had never seen such lines of exhaustion, such paleness and fatigue in the beautiful face. He saw her as he had years ago, and understood his own part in bringing about the change in her. He, in the grip of his madness, had done this to his wife, who was William's mother. William, who might be dying.

James' hand tightened on the revolver he carried in his belt. Baines' strong hand was quickly on his arm. 'Not yet, sir,' he hissed. 'Wait till they come past us. They must, and we can jump them.'

James paused, aware for the first time that he might actually have enjoyed killing Henriques. The man was a criminal who would only be hung if he were delivered to the authorities anyway, so perhaps there was even a certain illogic in handing him over. Daniel and he had come on this venture *solus*. It was the nature of their commitment. They had to see to themselves. To resolve their own affairs.

The *caboclos* had melted away, sensing that their part of the job was done. James, Daniel and Baines waited as the little party drew closer. Baines signalled to the two hands who were with them to give flank cover. Then, when Henriques and the women were at the closest possible point, Baines gave an animal roar and leapt out at the negro.

The negro was a huge fellow, but he was not as big as Baines. So few people were, James thought briefly, racing for another man. The negro went down to a shattering swipe, and Baines lifted his boot, striking Henriques full in the chest and driving him helplessly back. The hands meantime had appeared at either extreme of the group, causing the remaining man to scamper off wildly into the jungle.

Daniel raced for Elizabeth, catching her as Letty and Charlotte let go of her, confused and crying out at what had happened. Elizabeth slumped into her husband's arms. Her eyes blinked open.

'Daniel,' she whispered without the least surprise. 'Of course. I thought about you often, my dear. So often . . . ' And she slipped into smiling unconsciousness.

James, having felled his man, swung round. Suddenly Henriques was on his feet again, his rifle at the ready. James made to lunge at him, but Henriques already had his weapon trained on Letty and Charlotte, who had fallen back against a tree. They screamed in terror. James hurled himself at them, pulling them to the ground. The gun cracked and the bullet hit the trunk where they had stood, ricocheting away. James quickly got Letty behind him, protecting her with his body. He drew his revolver.

There was another ringing shot, but it exploded harmlessly into the air. Baines had thrust himself powerfully at Henriques, jerking the rifle he held upwards and delivering a punch to his midriff. The blow was so paralysingly severe that Henriques barely uttered a sound. His mouth fell wide open, and a blank, glazed expression entered his eyes. He crumpled in an ignoble heap at the foot of a tree.

James lowered his revolver. On balance, it was just as well he had not had to kill anybody. It would have been on his conscience. As the Indians were. The Indians from whose enslavement he had profited so grossly. Daniel had meantime gathered Elizabeth up in his arms. She slumbered peacefully, as in all probability she had not slumbered for a long time.

'James.' It was Letty's voice. His eyes travelled to her gaunt, dirt-streaked face. She was regarding him with what he could only take to be a kind of wonder. 'You chose to save me,' she said softly. 'Me . . . '

James did not know what she meant until his eye fell on Charlotte. She was lying on the ground at the base of the tree not far from them, sobbing in relief and shock. She had been quite exposed to the violence Henriques was offering. James obviously had not thought about it, but in a dreadful extreme, where the odds had been life or death, he had given the protection of his body not to his daughter, whom he loved so dearly, but to his wife, whom he had thought he did not.

James stuck the revolver back in his belt. It was necessary to recall the *caboclos*, who alone could get them out of this overgrown, oppressive place, and back onto the water, where there would be a clean wind to blow away memories of bitterness and foolish misunderstanding.

' . . . you mean he's actually succeeded?' enquired James in some incredulity. 'He took those rubber plants I shipped to England with him to Ceylon, and they've *grown* there?'

'Grown singularly well,' responded Letty. 'The rumour is they'll knight him for it. *Sir* Henry Wickham. And all because he has created a new rubber source within the British Empire. We're not in the hands of Brazil any more. Of people like *you*.' And she smiled indulgently.

'I'll be damned,' said James, still astounded by it. He looked round the expansive hotel lobby. He and Letty had in this building the grand room which until a few days ago had been occupied by the visiting opera singer, Chiara Santa. She had left Manaos rather suddenly, not happy about her performance, the manager had said. But in his opinion – and mind you, he would not breathe a word of this to anyone at all – there had been a gentleman involved. *Si, seguro.* A man of distinction. Who wished a certain discretion to be observed . . .

'James,' Letty began hesitantly. 'Now's as good a time as any to say it. I know I haven't replaced Anne in your life. That would be impossible. But – '

'Hush, Letty. Hush. That's the past now.'

184

The past. How quickly things became the past, she thought. Then the future – ? 'You'll go back to Liverpool now, James dear? Take up your affairs where you left off?'

Her husband sighed. 'If rubber is growing elsewhere, then I suppose that puts an end to making a fortune out of Manaos,' he returned. 'But if I go back to Liverpool, there could be considerable problems. Will you and Letty visit me in jail?'

'Don't talk stuff and nonsense,' scoffed Letty, for a moment the governess again. 'Jail. You've made a very great deal of money here. You'll be able to settle a lot of your debts at once. And people will be patient for the rest.'

'It's the end of the Onedin Line Ltd.'

'Not if you listen to Elizabeth.'

'Oh, Elizabeth . . . '

'And Daniel.'

'Daniel.'

James remembered how Elizabeth, in hospital after her ordeal, had wept and clung helplessly to Daniel for a long time. That had surprised him, for James had not thought there to be any longer an enduring affection between them. Elizabeth turned out merely to be suffering from exhaustion. As for William, their son, it had been announced that he would unquestionably recover. The convalescence would be long and demanding, as it always was in these matters, but he had his life. He had been spared the yellow killer.

'Letty . . . ' It was James' turn to be hesitant. 'When I – neglected you, I hope you realise it was a misunderstanding on my part. I was just so concerned to restore my fortunes that I didn't properly consider what applied to you. You must see that. I would never deliberately – '

'Hush, James dear,' cut in Letty, her heart light, her eyes smiling. 'Hush. That's the past.'

A week later, James stood with the now recovered Elizabeth looking down on the pontoons of the river at Manaos and the ships moored to them. The flying fox constantly brought

185

loads up from the vessels or lowered cargo to them.

'You'll be going back to your ship,' said James. 'The *Lady Elizabeth* has been brought to Para from Pernambuco. Your pirates did her no damage.'

'*Your* ship,' corrected Elizabeth, staring down at the activity on the mighty river. 'The *Lady Elizabeth* is your ship now.'

'Elizabeth, listen – '

'I tell you, that's the way it must be.' Elizabeth was firm and unyielding. 'I've got Daniel's agreement and the promise of finance for you with no strings attached. So that puts paid to the fear of bankruptcy. I've still got to get William's consent to the proposal, but I'm sure he'll agree. After all, he doesn't really want Frazer's. Not in any proprietorial sense. He hates the sea.'

Hates the sea. A chilling thought, James Onedin considered. His eyes were on the *Neptune*, moored at her pontoon. He thought he could make out the tall figure of Baines moving about the deck. He was not going to resign his command. They were loading a mixed cargo with which the ship was to return to England. 'Let me be very clear,' said James slowly. 'You will sell Frazer's for a token sum to the Onedin Line Ltd. In return I will guarantee financial participation to both you and William for life, and after our deaths our heirs and assigns to benefit in equal proportion from the business.'

'Quite simply, yes.'

'But damn it all,' expostulated James. The cross trees of the *Neptune* reared above every other vessel before them. 'What would I do with Frazer's? I'd be in steam.'

'It's got to come, James.'

'Not for me.'

'For the world?'

'I don't care about the filthy world.'

'You care about the world's people,' Elizabeth informed him. 'You've been to a lot of trouble to see that Henriques' slaves were released and adequately provided for. And you've given large donations to the Anti-Slavery League in England. Or was that all just to please Charlotte? Do you know that girl wants to study anthropology, James?' added Elizabeth. 'And she'll be able to, if you take over Frazer's and make a reasonable amount of money available to her. Things are changing for women these days. All the time.'

James frowned at her, curious a moment. 'How did you persuade Daniel Fogarty to guarantee finance for a venture I might be connected with, Elizabeth?' he asked. 'I'm aware the two of us are reconciled – if that's the word – but he's being remarkably selfless.'

Elizabeth's eyes twinkled as she gazed down at the sparkling water. It was a clear day, and for once the river looked almost attractive. 'There was the question of a certain opera singer,' she answered gently, patting her hair with a smile. 'Poor Daniel. He's quite repentant, and I believe him when he says there was never all that much to be repentant about. But William in fact came all this way and got ill because he thought I was being – ah – betrayed. Yes.' Her eyes danced again. 'Betrayal is a terrible thing. It may cost Daniel even more selflessness before it descends into the limbo of forgotten things. But he's a generous man, you know. He loves giving.'

James looked again to the *Neptune*. He seemed to see her great furled sails billowing, huge and proud as she ran before the wind. 'It's strange a man like me should fetch up boiling damned tin kettles,' he observed dourly. 'Even Iron Jack in his day used to say that I wasn't the kind to chug around the world in a puffing billy. I either stood still or I flew.'

'Well, it can be the same. It's a matter of the spirit now. Steam needs a spirit like yours to rise to the heights of which it is capable.'

'And what of you?'

'Oh, I'm just going to be a housewife after all,' answered Elizabeth simply. 'It's by choice, in case you think otherwise. Daniel knows I can always go off and be independent

187

again if he tries to reduce me to a part of the furniture as he did before. But I want to be with him in Australia. I want to be his wife.'

'The *Neptune* shall take you out there,' said James on a sudden inspiration. 'A last trip on a free ship, before the world gives up its arms to the manacles.'

'You think it as bad as that? As utterly hopeless?'

'We've lived through the best of all times,' James Onedin told his sister slowly. 'We've known how a man can be truly free, so free that he will acknowledge no master but the free wind. And we've learned and loved the mystery of the sea, which will be forgotten soon. Perhaps it's a mystery that was only ever meant to be understood by a very few. So we have been the chosen ones. The elect. And our names are written on the eternal oceans.'

He was high on the poop a moment as she rose and fell. His fellow seafarers, those who had also learned and loved the mystery of the sea, were with him. There was the creak of the halyards and the strain of the rigging as the mighty sails filled and bellied above. Across the vast water, a glowing sun sank red into the green. But he had no fear. If they journeyed on into the night, it was surely only to sail into the morning.

GENERAL FICTION

Δ	042697114X	Cyril Abraham THE ONEDIN LINE: THE SHIPMASTER	80p
Δ	0426132661	THE ONEDIN LINE: THE IRON SHIPS	80p
Δ	042616184X	THE ONEDIN LINE: THE HIGH SEAS	80p
Δ	0426172671	THE ONEDIN LINE: THE TRADE WINDS	80p
Δ	0352304006	THE ONEDIN LINE: THE WHITE SHIPS	95p
	0352302550	Spiro T. Agnew THE CANFIELD DECISION	£1.25*
	0352302690	Lynne Reid Banks MY DARLING VILLAIN	85p
	0352304251	T. G. Barclay A SOWER WENT FORTH	£1.95
Δ	0352302747	Michael J. Bird THE APHRODITE INHERITANCE	85p
	0352302712	Judy Blume FOREVER	75p*
Δ	0352305355	John Brason SECRET ARMY: THE END OF THE LINE	75p
	0352303441	Barbara Brett BETWEEN TWO ETERNITIES	75p*
	0352305916	André Brink RUMOURS OF RAIN	£1.95
	0352302003	Jeffrey Caine HEATHCLIFF	75p
	0352395168	THE COLD ROOM	85p
	0352304987	Ramsey Campbell THE DOLL WHO ATE HIS MOTHER	95p*
	0352305398	THE FACE THAT MUST DIE	95p
	0352300647	DEMONS BY DAYLIGHT	95p*

BARBARA CARTLAND'S ANCIENT WISDOM SERIES

0427004209	Barbara Cartland THE FORGOTTEN CITY	70p*
0427004217	L. Adams Beck THE HOUSE OF FULFILMENT	70p*
0427004225	Marie Corelli A ROMANCE OF TWO WORLDS	70p*
0427004233	Talbot Mundy BLACK LIGHT	70p*
0427004241	L. Adams Beck THE GARDEN OF VISION	70p*

† For sale in Britain and Ireland only.
* Not for sale in Canada. • Reissues.
Δ Film & T.V. tie-ins.

GENERAL FICTION

Δ	0426187539	R. Chetwynd-Hayes **DOMINIQUE**	75p
	0352303514	Magda Chevak **SPLENDOUR IN THE DUST**	£1.50*
Δ	0352395621	Jackie Collins **THE STUD**	85p
	0352300701	**LOVEHEAD**	95p
	0352398663	**THE WORLD IS FULL OF DIVORCED WOMEN**	75p
Δ	0352398752	**THE WORLD IS FULL OF MARRIED MEN**	75p
	0426163796	Catherine Cookson **THE GARMENT**	95p
	0426163524	**HANNAH MASSEY**	95p
	0426163605	**SLINKY JANE**	95p
	0352302194	Tony Curtis **KID ANDREW CODY AND JULIE SPARROW**	95p*
	0352396113	Robertson Davies **FIFTH BUSINESS**	£1.25*
	0352395281	**THE MANTICORE**	£1.25*
	0352397748	**WORLD OF WONDERS**	£1.50*
	0352301880	D. G. Finlay **ONCE AROUND THE SUN**	95p
	0352304073	**THE EDGE OF TOMORROW**	£1.25
	0352304995	Norman Garbo **THE ARTIST**	£1.50*
	0352395273	Ken Grimwood **BREAKTHROUGH**	95p*
Δ	0352304979	Robert Grossbach **CALIFORNIA SUITE**	75p*
Δ	035230166X	**THE GOODBYE GIRL**	60p*
	0352304359	Elizabeth Forsythe Hailey **A WOMAN OF INDEPENDENT MEANS**	£1.25*
Δ	0352305142	Peter J. Hammond **SAPPHIRE AND STEEL**	75p
	0352301406	W. Harris **SALIVA**	60p
Δ	0352304030	William Johnston **KING**	£1.25*

† For sale in Britain and Ireland only.
* Not for sale in Canada. • Reissues.
Δ Film & T.V. tie-ins.

GENERAL FICTION

		Heinz Konsalik	
	0352303956	**THE WAR BRIDE**	95p
	0427003210	**THE DAMNED OF THE TAIGA**	75p
	0352303883	**NATASHA**	95p
	0352304022	**THE CHANGED FACE**	95p
		Jeffrey Konvitz	
Δ	0352398981	**THE SENTINEL**	70p*
		Dean R. Koontz	
	0352301643	**NIGHT CHILLS**	85p*
		Andrew Laurance	
	035230412X	**PREMONITIONS OF AN INHERITED MIND**	95p
		Ellie Ling	
	0352304154	**THE FIRST SPLASH**	75p
		Pat McGrath	
	0352303328	**DAYBREAK**	95p
		Lee Mackenzie	
Δ	0352396903	**EMMERDALE FARM (No. 1) THE LEGACY**	70p
Δ	0352396296	**EMMERDALE FARM (No. 2) PRODIGAL'S PROGRESS**	70p
Δ	0352395974	**EMMERDALE FARM (No. 3) ALL THAT A MAN HAS . . .**	75p
Δ	0352301414	**EMMERDALE FARM (No. 4) LOVERS' MEETING**	70p
Δ	0352301422	**EMMERDALE FARM (No. 5) A SAD AND HAPPY SUMMER**	70p
Δ	0352302437	**EMMERDALE FARM (No. 6) A SENSE OF RESPONSIBILITY**	70p
Δ	0352303034	**EMMERDALE FARM (No. 7) NOTHING STAYS THE SAME**	75p
Δ	0352303344	**EMMERDALE FARM (No. 8) THE COUPLE AT DEMDYKE ROW**	75p
Δ	0352304103	**EMMERDALE FARM (No. 9) WHISPERS OF SCANDAL**	75p
Δ	0352304510	**EMMERDALE FARM (No. 10) SHADOWS FROM THE PAST**	75p
Δ	0352302569	**ANNIE SUGDEN'S COUNTRY DIARY** (illus)	£1.25
Δ	0352304340	**EARLY DAYS AT EMMERDALE FARM**	75p
		David Martin	
Δ	0352304286	**MURDER AT THE WEDDING**	95p
		Graham Masterton	
Δ	0352396164	**THE MANITOU**	70p*
	0352395265	**THE DJINN**	75p*
	0352302178	**THE SPHINX**	75p*
	0352395982	**PLAGUE**	95p*
	0352396911	**A MILE BEFORE MORNING**	75p*

† For sale in Britain and Ireland only.
* Not for sale in Canada. ● Reissues.
Δ Film & T.V. tie-ins.

Wyndham Books are obtainable from many booksellers and newsagents. If you have any difficulty please send purchase price plus postage on the scale below to:

**Wyndham Cash Sales
P.O. Box 11
Falmouth
Cornwall**
OR
**Star Book Service,
G.P.O. Box 29,
Douglas,
Isle of Man,
British Isles.**

While every effort is made to keep prices low, it is sometimes necessary to increase prices at short notice. Wyndham Books reserve the right to show new retail prices on covers which may differ from those advertised in the text or elsewhere.

Postage and Packing Rate

UK: 30p for the first book, plus 15p per copy for each additional book ordered to a maximum charge of £1.29. **BFPO and Eire:** 30p for the first book, plus 15p per copy for the next 6 books and thereafter 6p per book. **Overseas:** 50p for the first book and 15p per copy for each additional book.

These charges are subject to Post Office charge fluctuations.